VIC LEIGH

Buck

Stover Ranch Series Book One

This book was professionally typeset on Reedsy.
Find out more at reedsy.com

Contents

Acknowledgement

I want to thank my readers for always being willing to read my stories. You are the best and I thank you from the bottom of my heart.

To my ARC team…I don't know where I would be without you. Thank you so much for taking the time to read my book and review it for me. You all are priceless.

To my friends…Wow, I can't say enough about all the people that encourage me throughout each day, week, month, and year. You all are fantastic!

To Kyle and Kristie Stubbs…thank you both for allowing me to use your names, sort of, in this book. You guys are the inspiration of love and show that outwardly to the world. Kyle keeps everyone laughing, while Kristie keeps him grounded, as much as she can. Thank you both so much for allowing me to write this.

Note to Readers

Trigger Warnings

- Kidnapping
- Beatings
- Dead bodies
- Gore
- Violence

Prologue

Buck: Age 17

I jump in my Ford and head to the ranch. We have so many chores we have to do before we can go out and enjoy the night. I want to see Natalie tonight, so I've got to get busy.

We graduate this year, and I'm excited to get this school shit out of the way. Natalie is heading to college. College isn't for me because I'm a rancher and plan on taking over the family ranch with my brothers and sister.

My cell rings. "Yeah."

"Babe, you are coming over tonight, right?" Natalie asks.

"I wouldn't miss it for anything Nat. Your parents aren't going to be home, are they?"

"No, they are leaving in about an hour." This sounds promising.

"You sure you still want me to come over?"

"Kyle Stover... you know I do."

I laugh, "I will be there by seven."

"I have it all planned out. I'll see you soon." Nat giggles.

"I love you, Nattie… you're the best. I can't wait." I admit to her.

"I love you too, Buck, I'll see you tonight." I can hear the smile in her voice.

"Okay." I hang up as I pull down the long ranch driveway.

Our ranch is fifty thousand acres of pure Texas country. We run cattle, horses, and other livestock. It's a working ranch, and I love the work.

I finish my chores and run to the house to shower and clean up. Tonight, is going to be the best night of my life.

I finish showering and head down the stairs as my Pa comes up to me, "Son, you be careful out there tonight."

I look from Pa to Ma, "I'll be at Nat's. I'll be fine, Ma." I kiss her on the cheek.

I head for the door, and she swats my ass. I love my Ma, she's absolutely the best woman on earth.

She yells at me, "Love ya, son. Be safe… in all things."

"Yes ma'am." I head for my Ford and jump in. This is the night I've been waiting for since I was fifteen, and Nat and I started dating.

We said we would wait until we got married, but now, we know we love each other and don't want to wait. I know she's my future.

I pulled into Nat's driveway twenty minutes later.

She lives in a small house on Smithville's far side, going toward Big Springs. Her folks have a decent size spread, two hundred, twenty acres. They run a few heads of beef and usually butcher a cow each year for their freezer.

The house is cute, white with blue trim, a long front porch, and screen doors on the front and back. Her mom had planted some flowers along the front of the porch. But all I see is my girl standing on the front porch by the column that helps hold the porch ceiling up. She has the most beautiful smile I think I've ever seen.

Natalie's long dark hair flows down her back, her big brown eyes sparkle. When I look at her, her smile is as big as Dallas.

I walk up the path from the circle drive to where she stands, "Hey baby, you look good."

Her smile gets bigger, "Hey yourself."

She on has a pair of tan shorts showing off her long, tanned legs, a black tank top, and her bare feet with pink toe polish... she's so sexy. I grab her and pull her to me, her arms go up around my neck, and I lower my lips to hers. She tastes like strawberries and mint toothpaste. My tongue licks her lower lip, and she opens for me. I slowly delve into her mouth, tasting and exploring. Her tongue darts around mine, and we play dueling swords with our tongues. I slowly move my tongue in and out of her mouth, licking, tasting, and pulling her closer.

She pushes me back slightly and breaks the kiss, "Buck, we need to go inside. I fixed supper. I wanted everything to be perfect."

"Nat, if I have you, everything is perfect. I love you." I start to go back to her mouth, but she pulls back and slips out of my arms.

"Come on, let's do this right." She takes my hand and pulls me into the house.

I shut the door and lock it behind me.

Nat pulls me through the living room, which is modestly decorated in earthy tones, a fireplace, sofa, tables, and chairs make up the room. We make our way to the back of the house where the kitchen is. She has a small kitchen table set. The kitchen is a nice size with a center island, cabinets surrounding the back wall, a sink, stove, fridge, and the table in front of the bay window on the east side of the kitchen.

"It's perfect, babe, and it smells great. What did you make?" I ask.

"Spaghetti, garlic bread, and salad," she replies.

"Oh my gosh, my favorite. Thank you, sweetness."

"You are welcome. Now, sit down, and I'll put it on the table."

"You don't want any help?" I offer.

"Nope, let me do it. You've been working all day." She is so considerate and loving, how can you not want to be with her?

"Nat, so have you." I started to help.

She swats my hand, "Stop! Let me do this."

I throw my hands up and smile, "Fine, go for it."

I walk to the table and sit in one of the four chairs.

Natalie brings the bowl with spaghetti over, sits it in the middle of the table, and gets the bread and salad. There's a bottle of wine sitting on the table.

"What's the wine for? You know I don't drink."

"I know, I thought it would add to the ambiance." She giggles. I love that giggle. "I see."

"I put water with lemon in your glass." She knows me so well.

She serves the meal, so we sit and eat, making small talk about school, life, and what's coming next since graduation is only a few weeks away.

Once we finish dinner and the dishes, I look at her as she puts away the last dish.

"Natalie, you are the most beautiful girl I know." I pulled her into me. "I want you to know, we are getting married when you graduate from college. There isn't a question there, we've discussed it several times."

She puts her arms around my neck, "I know, and I want to marry you. I wish we could do it before I leave, but I know we can't."

I lower my mouth to hers once again, and as my tongue enters her mouth, she moans a soft, gentle sound. I pull her tighter against me, and I know she feels my dick against her stomach. It's hard as a rock.

She pulls back slightly, breathing a little heavily. "Come on."

She takes my hand and pulls me toward the stairs at the back of the kitchen. I've been to her room several times, but this time, it's different. She's my girl and has been my girl since we were fifteen. We reach her door, she pushes it open, and it's filled with soft twinkling lights all around.

"When did you do this?" I ask, looking around at all the twinkling.

"Today after school. It wasn't a big deal," she says like it was just like any other day.

"This," pointing around the bedroom, "is a big deal, babe. I love you."

That's when everything starts moving a little fast. She takes the hem of her T-shirt and pulls it over her head, tossing it to the corner of the room. Keeping her eyes on me the whole time. Then her shorts came off. I'm standing there stunned in silence because she's gorgeous. She's standing in front of me with a baby pink bra and thong. *Damn!*

"Nat, you look... amazing."

"Cowboy, you are wearing too many clothes." She giggles.

She comes towards me, pulls at the hem of my t-shirt, and pushes it over my head. I'm not sure where it lands. My eyes focus on the majestic woman in front of me. Her hand finds its way to the front of my jeans. She rubs my already throbbing cock through my jeans, and I think I may come before we even start.

"Babe, if you keep that up, we aren't going to get very far."

I bend down and kiss her temple, then her cheek. My mouth finds her lips and parts them with my tongue. She opens freely, taking my tongue, licking, and swirling around my mouth. As we kiss, I undo my belt, jeans, and slide my zipper down. I know this first time will be fast, but damn if I don't want this woman now.

I pull back and move my jeans down my legs, kicking off my boots at the same time. I'm standing in front of her with my red boxer briefs. The want to taste her is so strong. Her eyes grow dark and heavy as she backs up to the bed, taking my hand and pulling me with her.

"Nat, you sure about this?" I ask.

"Very. I want you, and I want you now," sounding needy and full of want.

"Yes Buck, I'm sure. You don't have to ask me again. I promise, I want this more than I've wanted anything in my life."

She sits back on the bed, moving to the center, resting on her elbows, and watching me. I make my way to the edge of the bed and kneel in front of her. I move my hands up her thighs and spread her legs open. I smell her arousal, and it turns me on even more. Moving my hands farther, I start kissing where my hands have been.

Her eyes are closed, and she moans again, only a little louder this time. As I move my mouth to her thong, I pull the small piece of material to the side. She's slick.

"Oh my God! When did you do this?" Looking at her pussy,

shocked that she would shave everything before tonight.

Her eyes fly open, "You don't like it? I was told guys don't like all the hair."

"Oh baby, I love it. But you didn't have to."

I start licking from the top of her clit to the bottom of her pussy. Damn, she tastes good. I had no idea this was going to be so good. When I return to her clit, she moans and grabs my head. Her hips start moving as my tongue circles around her clit, pulling it into my mouth and gently sucking.

"Oh, Buck!" Her breathing is getting heavier.

I assume that's a good thing and keep licking and sucking. As I lick down to her pussy, I delve my tongue inside, and she comes, hard and fast. *I wasn't expecting that... damn. So... good!*

"Oh…God!!! Yes!!!" she shouts out.

I don't stop. I keep thrusting my tongue into her wetness, and she gets wetter with each stroke. After she comes two more times, I begin to kiss my way up her torso, licking and kissing her stomach. I pull her bra down and begin to suck on her hard pearl-sized nipple, while pinching the other. It is a little awkward with this being our first time, but I manage.

Natalie's hands find their way into my hair, and she is holding me to her like she doesn't want me to stop. "Oh Buck… yes… that feels… amazing," she breathes out heavily.

I suck on both nipples, play with both, and move to her earlobe. As I move up, I position myself between her thighs. I still haven't taken off my boxers. I look at Nat, her eyes are closed, and she is enjoying this.

"Nat, open your eyes," I tell her, wanting her to watch me as I play with her sexy body. Her eyes flutter open, and she smiles a sexy-as-sin smile.

I reach down and push my boxers down, freeing my dick,

which is painfully aware of where it's going. This is the hardest it's ever been, and it's screaming to see some action.

Nat made sure we had all the necessities. She put condoms on the bedside table, several from what I can see. I grab one, rip open the package, and roll it down my length.

She's watching me and licking her lips. Damn, she's sexy.

I put my cock at her entrance and look into her eyes, "Natalie, this may hurt the first time. But it will get better, or so I've been told."

"Yeah, I've looked it all up on the internet. I'm good, I know what to expect." She puts her arms around my neck and pulls me to her, "Kyle Stover, make love to me."

Well, you don't have to tell me twice to do something. I begin to move slowly. Just the head of my dick starts to enter her tight wet pussy. *Damn, she's tight.*

She closes her eyes as I start to move in and out gently.

This is killing me to go slow.

Her pussy wraps around my dick and envelopes it like a bun wraps around a hot dog, so nice, tight, and sweet. As I start to move faster, I go deeper.

She moans, then she screams.

I stop, "Did I hurt you?"

"It hurt a little, but don't stop. Please!" The look in her eyes tells me to keep going.

I start to move slowly again, pushing through, and I feel the hardness before pushing hard one more time.

She screams out, "Oh, shit!"

I can't stop now, I keep moving. Her legs wrap around my waist as I push harder and faster.

Nat is now moving with me, "Yes! God, this is amazing."

My dick has a mind of its own because I start moving faster, pushing in and out harder and harder. "Nat, I'm not going to last long."

She's breathing heavily, "Don't stop! Keep moving... God, yes!"

I feel the warm sensation of her release curl around my dick, and I lose it. I come fast and hard. I pumped into her two more times and held still as I pushed hard one more time. I lift her up into me and hold her as we both start to come down from a high, I never knew existed. I feel both our heartbeats pounding in my ears as I hold her close, not wanting to let go. She has her legs and arms wrapped around me, not moving either.

I pull back slightly, and kiss her nose, "Well, that was amazing."

She laughs, "You can say that again."

"Well, that was amazing," I smile at her as my breathing is still trying to come back to a normal rhythm.

She slaps my chest, "Stop... you are goofy."

"Yes, and that's what you love about me."

"No, that's not what I love or rather, not all that I love. I love every bit of you. Everything about you, I love. This was amazing." She just can't stop smiling.

I push up onto my forearms and hover over her, "Yes it was. The most amazing thing I've ever done. I'm so glad you're mine, Natalie. I love you."

As I start to move, I begin to pull out of her.

"Wait! Go slow," she pleas.

I slow down and pull out slower, "Are you hurting?"

"No, just a little tender. But I'm fine." Natalie reassures me.

I roll to my side and pull her into my arms, holding her tight against me. I stroke her hair, down her arm, and hold onto her. "Natalie, how are we going to be apart for so long while you are off at school?"

"We'll make it work. I'll come home on every break, every holiday, every chance I get. It's a six-hour drive from here to there, we can make it work."

"God, you are perfect. I can't wait to marry you."

"I can't wait to marry you too, Buck. I love you!"

"I love you too."

At some point, we fell asleep holding each other.

* * *

Buck: Age 21

Nat is coming home this weekend, and I can't wait. She's been so busy, she hasn't been home in weeks. We've talked about wedding plans and where we want to have the wedding. Her dad came out to the ranch today to help Pa do some things and told me she would be home around nine that night. She got a late start and hit Dallas traffic right at rush hour.

I knew she was coming straight out to the ranch when she got back. We'd talked several times over the past week, making plans for her break this week from school.

I finish some stuff in the barn at six when I hear the chow bell. I'm starving and need to clean up before I head into the dining room.

I run to the house, to my room, and take a quick shower. Heading down to the dinner table, everyone but Morgan is there. He went off and enlisted in the Marines and is doing his first overseas tour of duty. I miss him, he's my best friend, and he's not here to discuss things with me.

Pa and Ma make us all eat dinner together at least four times a week. During the week, sometimes it's hard, but we all manage to get there if we can.

Mitch sits across from me, he's just younger than me. Brock is seated at the other end of the table near Ma. He's the baby boy, and it shows. Ma babies him so much it's pathetic. Jewel sits next to me, and Pa pampers her.

As the oldest child, I never got babied or pampered. I had to show all the others how to do shit around here.

Rooster is our cook and a damn fine one at that. He made Mexican tonight, enchiladas, rice, and black beans. The best meal around.

We sit at the table, eating and talking, when the phone rings.

Pa hates it when people call during dinner.

Ma gets up and answers the phone, "Hello… yes… one moment." She turns to Pa, "Kyle, it's for you."

"Damn it all, can't people leave ya alone while ya eat. This is bullshit." Pa is thoroughly pissed.

He picks up the receiver, "Yeah!" He's a little harsh. Then, his face almost goes white as we watch the phone call unfold. It can't be good without knowing who is on the other end, or what they are saying.

Pa hangs up the phone, "Joanie, take Jewel and Brock upstairs."

"What's wrong?" Ma is worried now.

"I'll tell you later. Right now, I need to talk to these two."

I look over at Mitch, "What did you do now?"

"Nothing that I know of."

I laugh. Mitch is not the family's troublemaker, but he has been in a few scuffles.

I look at Pa. "What is it, Pa? You turned white as a ghost."

Pa looks at me, "Come on you two, come with me."

Damn it, I want to finish my dinner. Mitch and I get up from the table and follow Pa to the living room. He pours three glasses of his good bourbon. *Shit, this must be really bad.*

He hands one to Mitch, one to me and takes one. He looks at us both, then looks at me, "Drink up. You are going to need it."

Mitch and I down what's in our glasses and then sit them down. I look at Pa. "Okay, out with it. Now I'm getting nervous."

"Son, you might want to sit down."

"I'm fine, out with it." I needle.

He looks at the ground, then at me, a tear rolling down his cheek, "I'm not sure how to tell you this son, but to just come right out with it. There was an accident on 35W."

My heart sinks, "And?"

"Son, Natalie was killed in a head on collision. A drunk driver at rush hour was going the wrong way. Hit her dead on."

I felt my legs buckle under me, and I saw white spots. I felt a hand on my shoulder and an arm wrap around my waist.

Mitch had me, "Come on Buck, let's sit down." He moves me to the sofa.

What the hell? What happened? She was fine a few hours ago when I talked to her. How? What?

My life was over. Or at least the life I thought I was going to have. I can't make it without her. I checked out.

Chapter One

Buck: Age 31

Getting up early on a working ranch in North Texas is just normal. I do it every day and have done it every day since before I could walk. My old man pushed us, so we would know what hard work was and wanted the best for us kids growing up.

Mornings like this are nice. It's cool, fall is setting in. I drink my coffee on the long-wide front porch of my childhood home and decide today will be a good day. Pa built the original house where it faced the east in the mornings. You can sit on the front porch and watch the sunrise. But if you were watching the sun come over the horizon, that meant you were late for work. Only women got that privilege on the Stover Ranch and even they were limited.

My ranch foreman approaches the porch. He has the glow of the horizon behind him. "Hey, you workin' today or just drinkin' your fucking coffee?" he firmly says.

Chapter One

Jack Holland is a raunchy old dude that's worked on this ranch longer than my thirty-one years of being alive.

"Yeah, old man. I was just admirin' the sunrise. That okay with you, you ole' fart?" I smile at him from the porch.

"I can still whoop your ass, if necessary. Damn punk kids. Come on, we got work to do."

I laugh. "I'm on my way."

Setting my coffee cup on the table just left of the front door near a swinging chair, I make my way down the six steps of the large porch.

I step up to Jack in about six steps, "What we got goin' on today ole' man?"

"One of these days, I'm goin' to whip your ass for calling me that." Jack says over his shoulder.

Laughing at the fact that he still swears he's going to kick my ass every day of the week, I just shake my head.

"I got Brett and Mike heading out to pastures forty-one to fifty checking fence. I got Bill and Nate working the shoots getting the inoculations done, and Jim and Dave are running to town to get the feed order."

"What about the boys? Aren't any of the Stover's working today?" I ask.

"You all need to get your head out of your asses. Ever' one o'ya act like the work around here gets done all by itself. I yelled at'm when I left the bunkhouse."

"Hey, seriously, how's Morgan fitting in since he got back?" My middle brother has had a time of it since he got back from the last conflict this damn country got us into. Morgan is a Marine, through and through.

Jack stops in his tracks and looks at me, "He's hurtin'. I can see it in his eyes, but he doesn't talk about it. He needs to talk it out and get it out of his system. But it's goin' have to be in his time."

I nod, "I'll go gettem' rounded up for ya. They should'a been up and working already."

"No shit, Sherlock. Laziest group of men I've ever seen. If ya can, send Mitch and Little Shit out with Brett and Mike to check the fences. I got a call last night a cow was roaming out on County Road. Gotta' be a break somewhere," Jack orders.

Confirming his order, I head to the bunkhouse. My brothers won't stay in the main house, they think it's fun to stay with the hired help. The bunkhouse sits a couple hundred yards from the main house, in front of the large red and white barn. I slam my fist on the door as I open it.

"Get up you lazy asses. There's work to be done," I yell throughout the bunkhouse.

"Shut the fuck up, Buck. Damn." My kid brother, Brock, is a pain in everyone's ass. Jack calls him Little Shit, and it fits.

"Jack wants you and Mitch to go out to forty-one with Brett and Mike, work the fences to fifty. You all should have been the first ones up and out there. This is our ranch dumbasses, and Jack got a call that one of the cows was out roaming County Road." They piss me off so bad it hurts.

Mitch grabs his hat, "Little Shit, was out late last night, some girl shit."

"Brock, when are you going to stop chasing skirts? You're damn near twenty-five. Get your head out of the pussy and figure out what the hell you are supposed to be doing," sounding like the big brother who has learned his lesson in that department.

"Unlike the rest of you asswipes, I like pussy. Seems to me, you all are a bunch of dicks that need to get laid more often.

Me, I'm doing fine in that area." Brock smiles as he grabs his tan Stetson.

I throw a chair toward him, "We have a fucking ranch to run around here, and you look like asswipes, all of ya. The hired hands are out first, every morning! Meanwhile, I have to come get your asses up and moving, just like when we were kids. Let's go!"

Mitch speaks up again, "Are they shooting the new heard that came in last night?"

I answer him, "Yeah, I'll help out Bill and Nate with that. You can head on over to forty-one, take Little Shit with ya."

"No problem." Mitch puts his brown Stetson on his head and heads out the door. "Come on Brock, let's go."

He looks at me and shakes his head, "You need to get laid and soon, you're an ass." He follows Mitch out the door.

Morgan stands from the bunk he was sitting on. "I'll go help Bill and Nate."

"Morgan, wait." I call out.

"Don't… I don't have time for you to try to psychoanalyze me. It ain't goin' a do no good anyway. I'll be at the shoots." Morgan walks out.

He is so troubled it's scary. I shake my head and follow him out. It's never dull on the Stover Ranch. I help with the inoculations, and after a couple of hours, my cell phone rings. It's Brock.

"Yeah," I answer.

"Hey man, we got a situation down here in pasture forty-five."

I stop and stand back from the shoot I was about to open, "What kind of situation?"

"Man, you gotta get down here and call the Sheriff's Department."

I turn around from the group and look at Morgan. "Call the Sheriff's Department for what? Spit it out, Brock."

"Man, we found a dead body. A man about thirty-five, no identification," Brock informs me.

"Fuck. Don't move. Don't move anything. Don't touch anything." I hang up the phone and call the Sheriff's Department, telling them what's going on and where to go. Then I holler at Morgan. "Morgan, come with me."

I run into the barn with Morgan right on my heels, and we start to saddle our horses. They are faster than the side-by-sides.

Morgan is curious, "What's going on?"

"Dead body found in forty-five," I spit out.

"Oh shit!" We head for pasture forty-five.

The sheriff's deputies get there about the same time, "What's going on out here?" asks Josh Trible, the lead deputy for the sheriff's office.

I look at Brock, "Where?"

Brock points to a small ditch about a hundred feet from where the men had been working on the fence. I follow the deputies over to the hole. Steven Holder, the other deputy, looks down, "I'll call the ME and Detective Brighton."

He walks off toward his patrol car. I've known both Josh and Steven all our lives. Josh is a year older than me, and Steven is a year younger. We all played football together back in the day, and they are good men to have on your side when things like this happen.

I look at Josh. "How long ya think it's been here?"

"From the decay, maybe a day or two. Not long. I'm surprised an animal hasn't gotten to it. When was the last time anyone was out here?"

"Nobody's been in these pastures for about a month." I look around at everybody, "Did y'all see anything suspicious when you got out here?"

They all nod their heads no.

Josh looks at everybody, "Who found the body?"

Mitch looks up at Josh, "I did. I had to pee. So, I went off to the side to do my business. That's when I found him."

Josh wrote in his notebook, "Did you touch anything?"

Mitch looks down at the ground. "Well, I had to see if he was alive. I checked for a pulse. I hollered at the guys, and they all came over, but nobody touched him but me. I checked to see if he had any identification on him, and he didn't."

Josh smirked, "The ME is going to have a field day with you. She can't stand it when somebody touches one of her bodies."

I look at Josh, "So fucking what? He wanted to see if the guy was still alive."

"Yeah, she's kind of an OCD type woman," Steven lets us know what to expect.

"I'll deal with her, don't worry." I gave him a disgusted look.

About an hour later, a side-by-side pulls up next to the other side by sides that were here, and a man and a woman steps out. The woman grabs a bag from the back. I recognize the man, it's JC Brighton. He's the lead detective in our county.

JC comes over and shakes my hand, "How ya doing today, Buck?"

"I was good until somebody said there was a dead body on my property," I huff.

JC smirks, "Yeah, that kind of puts a damper on things, doesn't it?"

"Yeah, kinda." I smile back at him.

"Who found the body?" he asks.

I nod my head toward Mitch.

JC looks at Mitch, "Did you touch it?"

"Just to check for pulse and identification."

As Mitch says that last part, the woman walks up and starts yelling, "You never touch a dead body. Ever!" she yells at us.

JC smiles, "Guys, I'd like to introduce you to Dr. Kristie Smith, North Texas leading ME.

She literally glared at Mitch as she continued her mouth vomit about preserving the integrity of the crime scene, and fingerprints, God, the woman would not shut up.

I yelled, "STOP IT!"

Everyone looked at me.

"Lady, I don't give a flying fuck who you are or where you came from, but you are not going to talk to my brother that way."

"You people have no idea how hard it is to…" she leads on.

I put my hand up, "Again lady, I don't give a fuck. Stop berating my brother for Christ's sake. He was trying to see if the poor guy was still alive."

She huffs, walks up to me, and points her skinny little finger at me, "Look here, you big overgrown kid, I have a job to do, and I'm going to do it to the best of my ability. And if that means putting someone in their place for doing something wrong, then so be it." Then she shoves that pointy little finger into my chest.

I grab her arm before she can move her hand away and growl out, "Don't ever touch me again, woman."

I can see JC and Josh snickering behind her. All the men turn their heads to keep from laughing. This little pint-size woman was taking on some pretty big men, and it didn't seem to faze her in the least. She backed up a little when I let her arm go, then turned and headed for the dead body.

I look at JC, "What the fuck was that?"

"That, my friend, is how she got to be where she is today. She's the youngest ME in the state, ever."

"I don't care if she's the daughter of the fucking governor, she's not talking to us like we're poor old cow people. We have a multi-billion-dollar ranch to run. How soon before you get that damn body off my property?"

"As soon as she is finished with her initial investigation. The wagon is on its way to pick it up now. To be honest, I will need to question each of you and whoever else is on the ranch."

I started to speak.

He put up his hand, "I know, but it's just a formality."

"You've got a dozen people on this ranch most of the time. I know it's a big operation, but I'll need to talk to everyone. Have you had any guests visit lately?" JC checks.

I look at Brock, who has decided to move to the back of the group to be out of the way, "Brock, you bring anybody home lately?"

All eyes were then on Brock.

"Oh, come on Buck, I'm not that bad. I brought home a couple of girls one time, and I'll never live it down." He shuffled his feet back and forth, causing the dust to start flying.

"You are the resident man-whore, just checking. Anyone else know of anybody on the ranch in the past few days?" Everybody just shakes their head, implying that they have not known anyone else coming onto the ranch.

Turning back to JC, Josh, and Steven, who has now joined again. "I'll meet you back at the ranch house, and you can question anyone that you need to. Let's get out of this Texas sun."

JC looks at me, "Sounds good. Thanks Buck. We'll meet ya back at the ranch house." They all take off toward the side-by-side they drove up in.

I look around at the men I have working the fence line. "I guess the work for now is going to have to be put on hold. Mitch, take my horse. You and Morgan head back to the ranch. Set the detective up in my office at the house. Brett, Brock, and Mike take one of the side-by-sides and head on back, see if Jack needs you in the corral. I'll wait on ME lady to finish. After they pick up the body, I'll take her up to the ranch. She rode out with JC."

Everyone nods in agreement and starts loading up the tools. Morgan and Mitch head out on the horses. They'll make it back, cutting through the land faster than JC and them will in an ATV.

I walk over to the ME lady and look down at where she's working. She's not a bad-looking woman. She's in a pair of tight jeans, boots, and a tank top. Her dark brown hair is pulled back in a loose braid, and her complexion is absolutely beautiful. *Where the fuck did that thought come from?* I shake that shit out of my head and clear my throat, "Is there anything I can help you with?" offering my help.

She looks at me from the ditch, "Actually, yes. Can you come down here? But be careful. Walk wide around the body, so you don't jeopardize any evidence. Josh and Steven will be back when they drop JC off."

I start down the slope, following the tiny boot prints I see in the dirt, they must be hers. "I didn't know they were coming back."

"Of course, they are. They have to gather the evidence

around the body, take pictures, you know, crime scene stuff. Surely, you've watched some kind of crime shows," she smartly says.

"Then what the fuck are you doing?" I must have given her a 'what the fuck' look.

"I'm the doctor. I have to collect evidence from the body prior to moving it. Then I'll perform an autopsy back in my lab. Here, pull up on his left shoulder and let me look at his back."

"Has anyone ever told you that you are one bossy heifer?" Sarcastically nudging at her ego.

She gasped, "Absolutely not. I'm a woman, not a cow."

Shaking my head at her and moving to where she told me to help, "Lady, that's not what I meant."

"Pull him up here, gently." She pulls something from the fabric of his shirt, puts it into a plastic bag, writes something on it, and puts it in her medical bag. "Okay, gently lay him back down."

I do and stand.

She proceeds to check his fingernails, hair, and ears everywhere. She works quietly and efficiently. I see dust coming down the trail, it's a side-by-side with someone following behind. Oh goody, more people.

The ME lady stands and hands me her bag, "Take that." Then she moves the exact way she came down. "Follow exactly where I am, we don't want any more prints than are necessary."

"God you are fucking bossy." I can't believe her boldness.

She gets to the top of the ridge, looks back at me, and sticks her hand out.

"What?" I look at her, confused.

"My bag, you big oaf." She rolls her eyes.

I shove the bag in her direction and leave her standing near the ditch. I walk over to meet Steven and Josh, shaking my head. I tell them that I'm heading back to the ranch and then head to the ditch.

I turn and look at the doctor, "You comin'?"

She huffs and gets back into the side-by-side, and I head toward the house. I'm not slow or easy on the ride, and I can tell she is displeased with me. Good.

Chapter Two

Kristie

I was working in my lab at the hospital in Howard County when I got Detective Brighton's call that a body was found near Big Springs, in a little town called Smithville.

I gather my necessary things for an onsite investigation. I'll have them bring the body back here for the autopsy.

Heading south from my office on highway twenty, I reach Smithville in about an hour and thirty minutes. It's a quiet small Texas town that looks like a western town from the early twentieth century.

I pull up to the station and walk into the stuffy little office.

A lady behind the counter asks, "Can I help you?"

"Yes, I'm Doctor Kristie Smith. I'm looking for Detective Brighton."

"Have a seat." She's not the most cordial person on the planet.

A few minutes pass, and I see the detective talking to someone. Then he heads over to where I am sitting. JC

Brighton is a nice-looking man, tall, not slender, but not fat either. His dark amber eyes sparkle as he smiles. He's wearing a pair of denim blue jeans and a nice polo shirt with the Smithville County logo on the upper right side of the shirt.

I stand, sticking out my hand, "Detective, it's good see you again."

"Good to see you too. You ready to head out?"

"Absolutely. Do you know anything yet?"

"I just talked to Steven Holder, a sheriff's deputy. The owners and a few ranch hands are out there plus another deputy, Josh Trimble."

"Has the scene been compromised?" I talk as we walk.

"No, not that I know of. We'll take the side-by-side out, it's in the middle of nowhere."

"That's fine." It's not like this is the first time I have had to go out in the middle of nowhere to inspect a body.

He points to a nice little ATV. I put my things in the back and jump in the passenger side, buckling in.

I look over at the detective, "JC, is everything okay? You're usually not this quiet."

"Yeah. Steven said one of the men touched the body. Now, before you go off…"

"They told them not to, right?"

"Well…"

"I'll take care of it when we get there," I'm furious. People are idiots. And I hate ranchers, cow people, and farmers. My ex-boyfriend was a rancher. He thought he knew everything, but then he lost his whole spread, gambling. Stupid fucking idiots.

We sit in silence as JC drives out to this God-forsaken middle-of-nowhere piece of dirt. Who the hell loves this shit?

26

It's stupid to be in the middle of nowhere. I need people. Okay, I don't need people. I'm pretty much a loner, but if I want food delivered at ten p.m., I pick up the phone, and it's there in less than thirty minutes.

As we pull down this long dirt path, I see several men standing ahead. I wonder which stupid imbecile touched my dead body. We stop, I grab my bag from the back, and follow JC to where the men are gathered. I walk to the group of men that seem to be having a nice chat when I hear one of them confess to touching the body.

"You never touch a dead body. Ever!" I'm furious. These cow people… ugh!

JC introduces me to everyone. One of the big men glares at me as I continue to tell the other man about the integrity of the crime scene. I can't remember everything I said because I was so mad. I remember pointing my finger at the biggest of them and telling him off, I think. I shoved my finger into his chest. Damn, it hurt. His chest was hard as a rock.

Walking toward the crime scene, I carefully step where I don't see any other evidence of tracks. I finally make my way to the body. My mind was not on this body but on the one standing at the top of the ridge. I hate cowboys. He's too damn good-looking for his own good. That strong jawline, and beautiful ice-blue eyes, I've never seen… stop it! I mumble to myself. I have to stop this. It's dangerous to think like that. The man is a craton, damn. I am working quietly when I hear something at the top of the ridge, and look. There he is God's gift to women. I bet he thinks he's something else too.

He asks to help, and I let him, against my better judgment, but I need the body lifted so I can see under him. The dead man looks to be in his late thirties, maybe early forties, with dark hair, there's something familiar about him, but I can't put my finger on it. I finish gathering what I need and tell the overgrown kid to walk carefully as we leave the pit this man found himself dead in this morning.

When I get to the top of the ridge, I see a side-by-side coming down the path with the ME van behind them. So far this morning, my intelligence has been criticized, I've been called a cow, and now I have to be left alone with the man-boy that thinks he's something else and ride back to town with him.

The deputies stop to talk to the man that has decided to be my guide for the day while I put my bag in the ATV. He's rude, hateful, and obnoxious. I've only met the man in the last hour, and I'm already disgusted with him and want away from him. After setting my bag in the back of the ATV, I get in the passenger seat and watch the hunk, I mean the man, get in the driver's seat. We head back down the path I came up only about an hour ago.

I assume he's taking me back to town, so I can meet the body at my lab. But he turns down another path and heads north from where we are. I look over at him, "Where are we going?"

"To the ranch house, where'd ya think?" He looks at me sideways.

"I thought you would take me back to town."

"Oh no, JC is at the house. He brought you, he'll get you back. I've got work to do. This has slowed my entire production day down."

"Well, heaven forbid your cows miss you for a few minutes." I give him my strongest go-to-hell look.

"Look lady, we do more around here than play around with cows." The man looked furious. "I have a multi-billion-dollar company here. We work our asses…"

I interrupted his rant, "I don't care about your damn cows, or your damn *company*. I've seen your like before. You treat people like they are beneath you and use them."

He looks over at me as we pull up a long drive to a beautiful house, "Lady, I have no idea who you have been mixed up with, but I assure you, we are not like that." He slams on the brakes, turns off the key, and jumps out of the ATV before I can say another word. He walks up the steps to a large, expansive, front porch as I just gawk at him. He turns around when he gets to the door. I was pulling myself out of the ATV.

He yells at me, "You comin'?"

Huffing under my breath, "Stupid man."

"What was that?"

"Nothing, I'm coming," I said in my most obnoxious voice. I hate being manhandled by some oversized cow*boy*… and I stress the word boy.

I walk up the beautiful farmhouse steps to the front door and follow him inside. The front of the house has a nice entryway with hardwood floors decorated in neutral colors, and plants adorn the two front windows on either side of the front door.

I look to my right, and he glares at me. "Come on."

Shit, this man is impossible. I follow him through another room I barely get a glimpse of because he is hauling ass through a door on the other side.

I walk in just behind him. What the hell was his name? Mr. Stover, that's right, "Um… Mr. Stover…"

"Call me Buck, everyone else does. Mr. Stover was my dad."

"Very well, Buck, is there a restroom I can use to wash up from being out in the fields?" I gesture my arm around.

He rolls his eyes at me, "Sure, princess, let me point you in the right direction." He steps out of the doorway and points to

29

another door in the back of the room we just barreled through, "There is a half bath right there. Help yourself."

"Thank you." I head to the restroom.

When I walk into the bathroom, I look at myself in the mirror, "What the hell is wrong with you today? Why are you letting this man get under your skin?" I shake my head, deciding to take a pee break. I do my business, wash my hands, and smooth down the flyaways in my braid. Taking a deep breath, I open the door, ready to face the man that has become the biggest pain in my ass.

I walk back to the room that Buck disappeared into earlier. JC is sitting at a large oak desk that faces the front of the house. The room is set up like an office, but it looks like it could have been a bedroom at one time. It's large and has bookshelves and filing cabinets around all but one wall. Against the front wall is a large, oversized leather sofa where two men sit. Buck is standing over in the corner.

The men stop talking when I walk into the room, and the two on the sofa stand and remove their hats. Buck rolls his eyes, and JC watches from his sitting position.

"I'm sorry, I didn't mean to interrupt, but I really need to get back to the lab, so I can start the autopsy on the John Doe," I look over at JC.

"Oh yeah, I forgot you came with me." He looks at Buck, "Do you have…"

Buck smiles, "Yeah, I have someone that can take the princess back to town."

JC shook his head, "Thanks Buck."

Buck comes up to me. "Follow me."

"Thanks JC, I'll let you know when I'm done." The two men sit on the sofa as I start walking out the door.

I heard JC say, "Thanks, Kristie."

I follow Buck back out the front door and down the stairs.

"Wait here," he says, pointing to the ATV. So, I wait.

Fifteen minutes later, I see Buck coming back from another house-looking building with a decent-looking man following behind him.

When they reach me, Buck says, "This is Brock, my little brother. He has graciously volunteered to take you back to your vehicle." Buck tips his hat and goes back into the house.

Brock is a nice-looking young man, with sandy blond hair and piercing blue eyes. He's wearing jeans, a t-shirt, and a cowboy hat.

I stick my hand out, "Nice to meet you, Brock. You were one of the men at the crime scene, weren't you?"

"Yes ma'am. You ready? I'll take you in the truck, less wind and dust." He starts for a dark grey Ford, and I follow behind.

He opens the door for me and gives me a large toothy smile. He might think I am interested in him, but that is the farthest thing from the truth. After shutting my door, he moves to the driver's side, gets settled in, and starts the truck. We move down the long drive, and before we reach the main road, he finally speaks, "So, you're a doctor."

Like that wasn't obvious, "Yes."

"Ya know, you are really pretty."

"Stop right there. I'm not interested in you or any other man." I straighten him right out. I don't want him thinking that I'm open to any man at the moment.

"Oh, sorry. I didn't realize you went that way."

I look at him confused, then shock spreads across my face, "No! God, I like men. I'm just not interested in dating right now. I had a boyfriend, he screwed me over, and I'm not ready for that."

"Well, ya know, we all have an itch we need scratched once in a while. Know what I mean?"

"No… yes… stop it! I'm too old for you, and I'm not interested in you."

"How could you not be interested in me? I'm a catch if you didn't know." His ego is apparently off the charts.

"Yeah, and you're full of yourself too. I'm not interested. Could we just hurry up? I need to get back."

He shook his head, "I can't believe my charming personality hasn't rubbed off on you."

"No offense, but you are way too young, way to forward, and way too much for me." I turn my head and look straight out the window.

"No problem. How old are you anyway?"

"You do not ask a woman that question! It's rude."

"Oh… I guess women my age doesn't care much. They tell me all the time." He smiles at me and turns back to watching the road.

We stay in complete silence after that last comment. Fifteen minutes later, he pulls up to the station.

"Thank you for bringing me back to town. I appreciate it." Opening the door, I start to step out.

"You're welcome, ma'am," he kindly says.

I turn back to Brock, "Why do all cowboys and farmers call women ma'am?"

"It's out of respect. If I didn't, my mama would haunt me for the rest of my life, and I ain't about to have that happen."

I smile at him, "I see. Well, thank you again, Brock. It was very nice of you to bring me to my car."

"If you ever decide you need that itch scratched, call me. I'm always looking for an older woman to teach me a thing or two." He smiles back at me.

"Good Lord, does your mama know you talk like that to women?"

"Oh no, she again, would come haunt my ass if she did."

I give a little laugh, "Then, stop it."

He smiles, "Yes, ma'am. See ya later."

"See you later Brock."

I close the door and move to my car, putting my bag in the back. I drive back to my Howard County lab, so I can perform the autopsy on the John Doe.

There is something weird about how this body was placed. I pull out my camera and look through all the screenshots I took of the body and crime scene. It looks eerily familiar, but I can't place where I've seen this one. I usually remember every crime scene. Maybe I didn't work the case, and that's why I can't remember. I don't know, but I will find out.

Chapter Three

Buck

I'm an asshole, I know this, everyone here knows this. Why did I have to be an ass to the pretty doctor? She's done nothing to me, so she yelled at Mitch. He's a grown man, he can take care of himself. Why the hell do I care that I yelled at her? I don't.

"Buck!" JC yells.

"What?" I yell back.

"Where the hell is your mind? Damn, I said your name four times, and you never once blinked."

"Sorry, I didn't hear you. Are you finished with the questioning?" I look over at JC.

He stood and moved to the front of the desk. When the hell had he moved?

"Yeah, for now. I'll wait for the ME report on the autopsy, and we may need to question others. Jack said there was a cow out on County Road. When was that?"

I look at him, "Last night, why?"

"And that's why you had men out there today, mending fences?" he asks.

"Yeah, if a cow got out... you think someone let it out?"

"Maybe. I'm still waiting to see what else we come up with."

"Okay. The only way to let a cow out back there, is through the fence or the gate that sits down on field thirty-one or through our pasture," I let him know.

"That's what I thought. The men found a break in the fence on forty-five, Mitch said. They were mending that spot when he found the body." JC looks at his notes as he remembered everything that went down this morning.

"JC, it's time for lunch. You wanna stay? Rooster always has a good lunch ready."

"Nah, I need to get back and start this investigation paper-work. I'll let you know what Kristie finds out after the autopsy."

"Thanks, JC. See ya later." I walk him out to the front.

JC gets into the side-by-side he rode out in, and I watch him disappear down the drive.

Rooster comes out of the house, wiping his hands on the dirty apron he wore around his waist. 'Rooster' Chet Black has been with the Bar S since I was a kid. Rooster looks me over, then steps to the triangle bell on the porch and rings it as he yells, "Come and get it!"

I smile and shake my head while looking over the space between the house and the corral. All my hands and brothers stop and shake dirt from their clothing as they walk toward the house. Eating at the big house for lunch every day when you were working, was tradition. One by one, they ascend the steps of the house and enter the large dining room between the kitchen and the office. The large wooden oak table sits in the center of the room with thirty chairs around it. Dad built it special so all the ranch people that work for us could eat lunch together.

When Mom and Dad were alive, mom thrived on cooking for the men. She would help Rooster, and the two of them would make sure there was enough food for everyone, and leftovers were sent to the bunkhouse for the men to snack on later.

As I sit at the head of the table, we give thanks and dig in. I sit and watch all the men around my table. This was my life, and I loved it. But lately, there seems to be something missing, I don't know. A man my age is usually married and has kids, but that wasn't in the cards for me.

My girlfriend during and after high school, Natalie, were set to get married after she returned from college, but she never did. A drunk driver killed her in a head-on collision outside Ft. Worth on her way back. What was worse is that was during her senior year of college. I haven't dated much since Nat. I loved that woman with all my heart, and I don't think anyone could ever take her place.

The dark-haired doctor kept invading my thoughts, and I have no idea why. She was terrible. She's bossy, mean and has nothing nice to say about anyone. But damn if she wasn't cute as a button when she got mad. I've got to stop thinking about her. So, I shake my head in an attempt to get those thoughts out of my head.

"What's wrong Buck?"

I look up and my brother, Mitch, looks at me. "Nothing, just thinking."

Brock pops off, "Yeah, I'm thinkin' 'bout that pretty little doctor that was out here. Ya know, she turned me down flat.

Told me she was too old for me." He laughs. "No one is too old for me."

"Stay away from that woman, she's trouble," I warn him.

"Nah, she's just another skirt to chase. She's pretty and knows it, I think," Brock says, with a hit of sarcasm in his voice.

I shake off his comment, he's probably right. "Any ideas who that man was Mitch found?"

"None. I've never seen him around here," Jack said.

Everyone agreed, and the conversation went on to something else. My mind keeps drifting back to the pretty doctor, damn it.

After a long day of working in the corrals, ensuring the cattle get inoculated, and finding a dead body on our property, I shower, change into my boxers, and jump into my big bed. As I lay there staring up at the ceiling, the pretty doctor lady comes back to my mind. What the hell is it about her?

I remember watching her walk and the sway of her hips as she moved across the dry land. Her nostrils flared when she got mad at me, but damn, she was sexy. I wanted to grab her by the neck and kiss that damn pouty mouth of hers.

Fuck, now my dick is hard. What the hell is wrong with me? You would think I was a teenage boy. Of course, I haven't had sex in so long, I can't remember when or with who. Oh yeah, that pretty blonde at the rodeo last June. Damn, that was a year ago. No wonder I'm lying here with a hard-on. Shit, I need to get laid. Maybe Shithead can help me out. He has women all over the place. Nah, I don't want my little brother's leftovers.

I reach under the covers, pull my dick out of my boxers, and start stroking it. The damn doctor comes back to my mind. I can imagine her lips wrapped around my hard cock, while I face fuck her. My hands in her dark hair as I pound away, watching her eyes as I shoot my seed down her throat. Fuck, my hand moves faster and harder the more I think about that woman. The next thing I know, I'm coming all over my stomach.

Son-of-a-bitch! I lie there for a minute, then get up, go to my ensuite bathroom, and clean myself off. I stare into the mirror after washing my hands, "You, my friend, are fucked up." I turn down my head and go back to bed. My sleep is restless, and I'm not sure I slept much. It's been a week since the dead body incident, and still I haven't slept much all week. That damn doctor keeps coming to my mind every time I lay down.

I head to the barn to do some of my chores, and JC comes driving up. As I step off the last step, he stops in front of the house.

He gets out of his car, and we shake hands. "What's up, JC?"

And damn it, that woman doctor steps out of the other side of the car as I shake hands with JC.

"Doc here has some questions for those that were at the scene before she got there." He points over at Dr. Smith.

I roll my neck back and look up at the sky, wondering what in the world I did to piss God off this time.

"Mr. Stover." Kristie barrels up to me like she's pissed.

"Doc," I almost snarl back at her.

"I would like your cooperation, if possible."

Damn, she's snooty, "I'll do my best to accommodate your highness." My hands are on my hips, and I'm about to get pissed off. But I really want to kiss that damn mouth of hers.

She huffs, "You are a rude, egotistical, self-centered..." she starts mouthing off.

"Now look here lady…"

JC steps in, "Okay you two, stop. Buck, can we borrow your office?"

"Yes," I agree.

"Can you gather those up that were at the scene before Dr. Smith, and I arrived?"

"Yes." I'm still staring at the princess doctor while answering JC's questions.

"Fine, Kristie, come on." JC heads up the steps.

Kristie huffs at me again and then follows JC up the stairs.

"My lord that woman is insufferable." I head to the barn to gather the men.

Walking into the barn, I see Mitch, "Hey, that pain in the ass doctor wants to see you and the others that were at the fence line that day y'all found the body. She's in my office. I'm heading to check cows."

"You aren't staying? Do we need a lawyer?"

"I'm not staying, that woman is a pain in the ass. I don't think you would need a lawyer. If you did JC would have said something. He's not questioning anyone; she is, for some unknown reason."

"You like her. Damn Buck, it's been a long time…"

"Fuck you, asshole. Just get your asses in my office and talk to the damn princess," I demand.

Mitch starts laughing and puts his shovel down, "Yes sir, big brother. You should maybe be nice to the woman. She's a looker."

"Fuck you!" I head to saddle my horse. I need to get away from here.

I walk back to the stall where Cocoa is. "Hey girl." I pet her nose as she sticks it out of the stall door.

"Where ya headed?" Jack walks up next to the stall, putting his hand on Cocoa's neck. Cocoa is a chocolate brown purebred quarter horse. She is one of the best-cutting horses and prettiest in the state. She has a black tail and mane, a small white streak down her nose, and white boots around her hooves.

"I've got to get away from here."

"Mitch said the pretty doctor lady was back." Jack smiles at me.

"Yes, the princess is using my office to question the men, *again.*"

"Want some company?"

Chapter Four

Kristie

I was in the office when JC's phone went off. He steps out of the room, and I finish talking with Mitch Stover. He didn't have anything to add. I just needed to ensure I didn't miss anything before releasing the autopsy to JC.

JC comes back in. "Buck and Jack found another body, pasture thirty."

Mitch stands. "What the fuck is happening around here? Do I need to round up the boys?"

JC looks at me, then back at Mitch, "Nah, I think Doc, me, and maybe one other can handle it."

Mitch nods and heads out the door.

JC looks at me, "It's a different location. Buck and Jack were checking cows, and that's when they found it. He's roped off the area where the body is so no one will get back there."

"Shit…really? At least he's finally using his head for something besides a hat rack. Stupid cowboys. What is happening?"

Kristie asks.

JC chuckles, "No idea, I'm calling in some help on this. I'm going to go check on the horses we are riding out there on."

"I need to finish up here and I'll be out there shortly."

JC heads out the door.

What the hell is going on? Two bodies in a week on the same ranch, that is not a coincidence.

I walk out of the house, and the cute smartass cowboy that took me back to town the other day is standing there with a shit-eating grin. What is it about cowboys that makes them think that they're God's gift to women?

"Doc, couldn't stay away, could ya?" Mitch walks up saying.

"Well, since there's been another body found, no I couldn't."

"Buck called and I'm supposed to take you out to the pasture. He told me to bring you straight out there as soon as possible."

"Did he now? Well, I'm waiting on JC, then we can go out together."

"JC isn't sure of which pasture it is, I'll have to take ya. He's in the barn getting the horses ready."

I shake my head, "Fine, whatever. I need to use your bathroom if that's okay."

"Sure enough, ma'am. Come on in. Do you remember where it is?"

"Yes, thank you." I move through the familiar dining room to the back bathroom, waiting for JC to get the horses ready. I don't want to spend more time with that young pup than I have to.

As I finish washing my hands, I hear voices in the other room. When I open the door, JC comes back in.

"There you are. Are you ready? The horses are ready."

"Um… horses?" I look at him with a panicked look. It didn't

register with me that we were actually going to take horses. I hate horses!

"Awe… come on darlin', you can ride with me. You afraid of horses?" Brock asks.

I give JC a look of pure terror.

"I've saddled the tamest horse they have. And Brock, you don't need to go. This one doesn't concern you." JC comes to my rescue, thank goodness.

Brock tips his hat as he walks out of the room, giving me a smile and a wink.

I look at JC, "That kid is incorrigible."

JC busts out laughing, "He's chased every skirt between here and Dallas Doc. That's just Brock. Come on, you can ride beside me, and I'll make sure you are okay."

I follow JC to the barn, where three horses are saddled. "Who else is going with us?"

"Morgan. He's going to make sure we get to the right pasture and all. I'm not sure exactly where it is."

"Oh, okay, he's fine. I didn't want that kid going. He's a mess."

"That he is." JC chuckles. He goes to the horse's left side with me and helps me up in the saddle. He looks at me, "If you are nervous, the horse knows it. Just try to be calm and stay settled down."

Morgan looks at me. "Ma'am, she's the gentlest horse on the place. She will be fine, just don't try any funny stuff, like trying to run or anything."

"Oh, don't worry, there will be no running." I assure him.

JC hands me my medical kit for the onsite evaluation and helps me strap it to the saddle.

"You just stay between Morgan and me, and you'll be fine."

"Thanks JC." I smile at him, letting him know I'll try.

We head out and my horse follows Morgan with JC right behind me. Someone opens a gate, and we walk our horses through.

It seems like we have been riding for hours, but Morgan told us it had only been a little over an hour, and we should arrive at the scene shortly. I hope so, my butt and legs are killing me. I hate horses and the country, and it's ridiculous that people live like this.

My horse moves slightly to the right, trying to get around Morgan.

"Ma'am, you'll need to stay back."

"Well, that would be great if you could just tell her that. I'm not doing anything."

"Tighten up the reins a little, she'll pay attention," Morgan instructs.

"The what?"

"The reins. The straps you are holding in your hand. Tighten up on them a bit and she'll back off."

I pull back on the reins and the horse nearly backs up over JC.

JC yells, "Whoa, there. Not on me."

Morgan is yelling, "Not so hard, let up," he tries to help.

This horse has a mind of her own. She's either backing up faster or trying to go forward quickly, and I don't do fast on a damn horse... this is ridiculous. I let the reins go slack. She moves forward, I pull back, and she moves around, like a yo-yo only side to side. Morgan is waving his hand in front of the horse's face, which is pissing her off because she is starting to stomp.

"Oh shit!" The horse rears up on her hind legs, then plops

back down. We take off in a fast gallop, and my arms are flailing everywhere. I'm trying to get the horse to stop, but she doesn't seem to want to listen to me. "Stop? Hey! Quit that, come on!"

Just about the time I think I'm going to land in the water just ahead, I feel a strong-arm wrap around my middle and pull me from the horse.

When I look to see who it is, it's Buck. Damn.

"Where the hell did you come from?" I look at him bewildered.

"I heard you screaming and yelling and didn't want you to frighten the herd, so I made my way over here from the other side of the pond. You okay?"

"Yeah, thank you. I didn't know what I was doing," I admit.

"You should never ride a horse unless you know the animal. They are very intuitive to your reactions and feelings. You have to stay calm."

The horse comes to a stop, and he slides me off the horse, then he slides down.

"I'll have you know, I had no idea what I was doing but was told it was the only way to get back here. Otherwise, I wouldn't have ridden that damn wild beast."

He smiles, "What? Molly is the gentlest horse on the place." He rubs the horse's neck.

His smile is intoxicating. I hadn't seen it the last time I was here, he was an ass then.

"Well, she seems to have a mind of her own," I explain.

The smile vanishes as fast as it shows up, "Look, you can walk the rest of the way up to the body. It's up there."

"Thank you." I'm so relieved that it is not much farther and riding the damn horse was not an option anymore.

JC hands my medical bag to me, and I start walking up the slight hill to the group of trees. As I walk up, I see where Buck attempted to rope off the area. He actually didn't do a bad job. I take my phone out and start taking pictures of the area and the body from different angles. Once I got the photos taken, I start working on the body. It's placed strangely, leaning up against the tree, and sitting like he's watching over the pond and cows.

JC comes up behind me as I finish the work on the body, "What did you find?"

"It's weird. He's sitting here like he's watching something. His throat has been cut from ear to ear. I'm not sure why he would be sitting like this."

JC took some pictures as well. "I'll have to get the guys to rig up a stretcher to get this guy out of here. I've got a forensic team coming from the state department. They want to see both sites and see if they can gather some evidence. Buck is going to have the men bring some cattle panels out to surround the area so that it's not tampered with before they get here."

"JC, what is going on around here? Why are bodies being left on this ranch? Do the Stover's have any skeletons we need to know about?" asking him due to the fact that this is the second body in a very short time.

"Nah, it's just a big ranch. How long has this one be dead?"

"At least twenty-four hours. Maybe a little longer," I estimate.

JC walks around the area looking for clues as I finish my assessment.

"How is a team of forensics going to get back here? On horses?" I look skeptical.

"Yes, that's how things are done around here. You'll get used to it."

"Oh, I don't think I'll ever get used to this kind of life. As soon as you can get the body back to my lab, I'll get the autopsy completed."

"What did you find on the other…" JC starts to question me when we heard gunshots.

"What the fuck?"

JC pulls me behind a tree, and I glance around him to see what's happening.

Buck, Morgan, and Jack are riding hard toward our location. Each of them has a gun in their hand. They all dismount and head for us. They all find a tree to hide behind and look around the tree to see if they can see who is shooting at them.

I look over at Buck, who is behind the tree next to me. "What the hell is going on?"

"No idea, stay hidden behind that tree," Buck insists.

I do as I'm told.

The next thing I know, a shot is fired, and the bullet hits the tree I'm hiding behind. Morgan is on his phone, Buck shot at someone shooting toward us, Jack was doing the same, and JC was trying to keep me hidden.

Morgan yells over the gunfire, "The chopper is on the way with more fire power."

Buck nods, "Good, who the fuck are these assholes and what the hell are they doing on our property?"

"No idea bro, no idea." Morgan says.

Buck looks over at me, "Helps on the way, hang on."

He must have seen the fear in my eyes. It feels like hours since the last gunshot rang out. JC said it had only been about twenty minutes though. I heard a whirring sound, and it was getting louder. Then we hear what sounds like motorcycles.

Buck says, "Fuck, dirt bikes. There has to be at least five that

I heard start up."

Morgan agrees with him, "I hear Mitch coming."

As I look around the tree to see what they are talking about, a helicopter crests the mountaintop just over the western ridge of the property. *A helicopter? They made me ride a damn horse, and they have a helicopter?* I'm fuming.

I'm also shaking and unsure if it's because I'm mad or scared.

Buck looks at me, "Are you okay?"

I put my hands on my hips and start to yell at him, "Why the hell did I have to ride a fucking horse if you have a helicopter?"

"I'm not sure. If you'll remember, I was here waiting for you to get here. I'm not sure who told you to ride a horse."

I glare at Morgan, "Your little brother is the one that suggested I ride a horse."

He hides his smirk with his hand, "Yeah."

By the time the chopper lands, the shooters were long gone.

Mitch steps out of the chopper with a gun and four other men with weapons. Good lord, what have I gotten myself into around here? This is ridiculous.

Chapter Five

Buck

As I stand there watching this adorable, pain-in-the-ass doctor yell at my brother, I can't help myself. My dick gets hard. Fuck, she's cute when she's mad. *Damn, where did that come from? I ask myself once more. She just keeps coming into my thoughts. I've got to get over her, but I can't.*

I walk over to see if I can bail my brother out of this mess. "Brock, did you convince the Doc here that she needed to ride a horse?"

He has a big fucking grin on his face, "Yep, sure did."

I look at him shaking my head, "I'll take care of you later."

I grab the Doc by her waist, lift her tiny body, and pull her away from my brother, knowing that if she stands there any longer, she might hit him. Which would be funny, but we have a murder to solve here. So, I haul her ass over by JC and put her down.

"You brute, what the hell are you doing to me? Leave me

alone!" She slaps my arm. I just glare at her. All this time, JC and the other men are standing around laughing at the entire situation.

"JC, we've got these murders. What are we gonna do? We gotta get them solved. Why are people coming on my property and dumping dead bodies?"

"Man, I don't know. The investigative team has pulled in, so we'll make sure we get everything that we need before we take the body. Doc, you got everything you need here?" JC turns to her.

She puts her hands on her hips, glaring at JC, "Yes, I've got everything I need. Thank you very much."

"Okay, who can take her back in the chopper?" JC asks.

I look over at Mitch. Then I look at Brock. Then I look back at her, "I'll take her. Make sure my horse gets back to the barn."

There's no way I'll let either of my brothers take care of this woman.

"Doc, you ready?"

She huffs, "Yes, get me out of this godforsaken place."

I look around at all the men, and all of them are either laughing, smirking, or shaking their heads. I throw my arm out for her to follow to the helicopter.

She storms off without saying a word.

I mumble, "Women."

I make my way to the chopper and help her into the copilot seat. Then I make my way around to the other side and get in. I look at her and hand her headphones. "Put this over your ears, so we can talk to each other while flying."

She glares at me and snags them out of my hand. She puts them on her ears. "What if I don't wanna talk to you."

"I heard that."

"Shit."

"I heard that too. You better be nice. I'm flying you back to the house. I could make you ride the horse back." I give her the option, knowing damn well she won't want to ride.

Again, with the glaring eyes, the beautiful copper glaring eyes. *What is this woman doing to me? Fuck. I haven't had this feeling for a woman in a long time.*

I flip switches and start the helicopter. Putting my headphones on, making sure she can hear me through the speaker, "Can you hear me, okay?"

"Yes."

"Alrighty then, here we go." I pull back on the stick, and we head back to the ranch.

After about two minutes, I finally speak, "Doc, if we keep meeting like this, something's going to happen. You're driving me crazy."

"What do you mean I'm driving *you* crazy? I haven't done anything. I came out here to investigate the dead bodies. There's two now. What do I do with that?" questioning what one thing has to do with another.

"I mean, you're driving *me* crazy."

She looks at me. I stop watching her. My dick twitches again. I can feel her staring at me. I think she's trying to burn a hole through me.

"Just exactly what do you mean by driving *you* crazy?"

"Oh, never mind. Why are women so dense?"

"I'll have you know, I'm not dense. I am a very smart, well-educated female. It is men like you that drive *me* insane."

"How about we not talk the rest of the ride?"

"Fine by me."

Ten minutes later, we are flying over the top of the barn,

heading to the helipad. I gently lower the chopper down and kill all the switches. I take my headphones off and hang them in the hangar. I glance over at her, "Look, Doc, I think we got off on the wrong foot here."

"Ya think?" she says, sarcastically.

"See, now what is it with that attitude?"

She hangs her headphones up on the hanger, and then opens the door stepping out. I jump out of my side and walk around.

"Look, we have to work together, apparently. Why is it that you have a difficult time looking at me and talking to me like I'm a civilized human being and not like a piece of dirt that you're walking across?" I'm almost in her face, and I feel my blood pressure rising by the second.

She puts her hands on her hips, stares at me, and doesn't say anything. She just stares at me.

God, she's gorgeous. Her long dark hair and copper eyes with a ring of yellow around the iris, so fucking gorgeous. Her chest is heaving. I can see the top of her breasts over her tank top. What doctor wears a tank top and a pair of shorts to a body sighting? I shake my head and turn to walk away.

I head for the barn. I hear her coming up behind me. I keep walking.

"Hey!" She yells at me.

I don't respond, I keep going.

Again, she yells at me, "Hey."

I turn around abruptly, and she runs smack dab into my chest. I catch her with my hands on her upper arms. I'm looking at her. She can't be more than five-five or five-six. I'm breathing heavy, she's breathing heavy. Her hands are on my chest. *God, she feels good. It's been a long time since a woman affected me this way, I think again. I could fuck her. I could fuck her and get her out of my system.*

She's staring into my eyes.

My eyes lower to her plump lips. The next thing I know, my mouth is on hers.

My tongue is dueling for dominance over hers, even after all that fighting and fucking nonsense.

She moans. She fucking moans.

God, it sounds good. I pull her closer. I feel her arms go up around my neck. She wants this as much as I do, and she wants me. Fuck yeah.

I come to my senses and pull back. I don't let her go, however.

"Fuck doc. You can fucking kiss."

She blinks a few times.

"Don't think, what did you feel?"

She shakes her head but doesn't say anything. Her hand is searing heat through my shirt. That delicate hand is resting on my chest, but she still looks lost.

My hand goes up to cup her cheek, resting where my fingers are in her hair. I force her to look at me, "Doc, come on. You felt it too, didn't you?"

"I don't know what I felt." She pushes on my chest and takes a step back.

My hands fall to my hips, "Look, I'm sorry. I guess I misread the signals. It won't happen again."

I turn back toward the barn and hear her on my heels. What the hell is this woman doing? I can't be around her right now. She's driving me nuts!

As I make it to the barn's back door, she moves beside me. "Look, that took me by surprise. I'm not a fan of cowboys. They tend to lovem' and leavem' and I'm not that kind of woman."

I open the barn's back door and enter without saying a word. Kristie is right behind me, "Did you hear me?"

I move to my office, which I keep in the back section of the barn. I open the door and know that she is still following me. I walk in and start to shut the door in her face when she puts her hand on the door, keeping it from closing.

"Look, maybe we did get off on the wrong foot. But I have a job to do and… well… shit… cowboys make me nervous."

Looking down at her, I manage to get out some very harsh words, "Then leave. I wouldn't want to make you nervous."

Again, she's staring at me with no words. She looks like she's pouting, and those damn lips are begging me to take them again. Fuck! I grab her wrist, pull her to me, and my mouth is on hers again… hard, fast, and desperate.

I pull her inside the office, not breaking the kiss, kick the door shut with my boot, and pull her as close to me as humanly possible. Her arms wrap around my neck, she's pulling me in, and I'm not going anywhere. My hand moves to her delectable ass, cupping her ass cheek and squeezing. I move my other hand to the other ass cheek and do the same, pulling her hips into my now extremely hard dick.

A moan escapes her, and I swallow it.

I break the kiss and move my lips down her neck, nuzzling her ear lobe.

The next thing I know, she is clawing at my shirt, trying to get the buttons undone. I move my hands to her waist and reach under her tank top, feeling her luscious soft skin under my rough fingertips. My hands move up, pulling her tank top up as I go, exposing the most delectable breasts I've ever seen in my life., I need to be skin to skin with this woman.

"Doc…"

Chapter Five

"Mmm?"

My shirt is finally open. Her breasts are perfect, round, and heaving from our breathless kisses and touches.

"God Doc, you are so fucking beautiful." My lips are on hers again.

Her hands reach the button on my jeans, feeling her undo them. She pushes them down, and I kick my boots off as well as my jeans.

I pull back from the kiss and stare into her eyes, "Doc, I need to know something."

She clears her throat but looks at me through hooded eyes, "What?"

"Do you want this? Do you want me?"

She shakes her head, "Yes."

Putting my hands in her hair, I crash her lips back to mine. Hot and wet, my tongue delves deep, roaming fast and hard. We pull back for a moment, and my head is on her forehead, panting for air.

She steps back from me so that I can't touch her.

"Wait," she breathlessly says.

Then, she gives me a seductive smile, and those copper eyes turn darker. She's standing in my office in a bra and jean shorts, staring at me with a look of want. She moves her hand to the button on her shorts, then undoes the button and slowly unzips her shorts. This is torture. She's moving so slowly.

A smile crosses her lips, and the shorts fall to the floor. No fucking panties… damn.

"Oh my God woman, you are… fucking amazing."

She moves her hand behind her back and undoes the clasp on her bra, letting the straps slip down her arms and fall to the floor. I think I may die, this is amazing. She's standing in front of me with her gorgeous, tanned, naked body. She moves her hand to her hair and pulls out the ponytail holder that is holding it back. Her brown hair falls down and flows down her back to nearly her waist.

Where the fuck did this glorious creature come from? She's so fucking amazing.

Her body is slim, but not too slim. It curves in all the right places. I check her out from the top of her head all the way down, roaming my eyes. When I get to her tits… oh my God, the best-looking tits on earth. Her nipples protrude, begging for my mouth to be on them.

Her hands are on her hips as I continue my visual perusal of this magnificent woman. Her flat stomach leads to her pussy. Oh yeah, she's slick. Her legs are long and lean. She works out, that's for sure.

My eyes roam back to hers, "I don't think my dick is going to get any harder than it is right now."

She laughs, "Then what are you going to do about it?"

I want this to last, but I also want to ravage her body and make her mine. *What the fuck? Why would I think that? I'm in the moment, that's all.*

She starts to move toward me, and I think I may be drooling. Her hand reaches my chest, and she pushes my shirt off my shoulders. It cascades down my back and hits the floor.

"My oh my, Mr. Cowboy. You are one fine looking man."

I give her my best grin. My hands start to go to her breast, and she shakes her head. "Not yet. We need to be more… even."

My dick is standing at attention, and she can see the head peaking up over the waistband of my boxer shorts.

She moves her hands to the waistband of my underwear, puts her thumbs in the sides, and painstakingly slow, she moves them down my legs.

My dick springs to action. I'm not a small man. My dick is hard as steel and hurting to get inside this woman. She licks her lips, kneels in front of me, and shit fire. She puts her tongue on the head of my dick, licking the pre-cum, swirling it around before taking me deep into her throat.

I about come undone at that point. I feel the head of my cock hit the back of her throat as she starts to bob up and down on my dick, gently sucking and licking my shaft with that beautiful mouth of hers. I moan out loud, knowing that she is actually enjoying this.

I put my hands in her hair. I can't take it anymore. I pull her up from the floor, "I don't want to come yet, and if you keep doing that, it will all be over way before I'm done with you. Damn woman, you are… incredible."

The look in her eyes tells me I've done something wrong, "Sorry, I thought you would like that."

"Don't you ever fucking say you're sorry for sucking my dick baby, you are unbelievable. I just want to come in you, not your mouth."

Her mouth forms an 'O' in understanding.

I cup one of her breasts as my mouth finds the other, pulling her nipple in between my lips, I lick and suck her nipple until she moans.

"Buck, please…"

I move to the other nipple and give it just as much attention.

Her head is thrown back, and her hands are on my back, pulling me closer to her.

I pull off her nipple, "I need to taste you. I want that pretty little cunt of yours."

My mouth is on hers again as I back her to the leather sofa

I have in my office. It's usually used for the men to come in and relax for a few minutes. Today, it's going to see a lot more action.

I lay her on the sofa, put one leg on the back, and the other on the floor. "Baby, you are so gorgeous, spread out for me like that." I kneel, putting my hands under her hips, pulling her close to the edge, and my tongue finds that perfect little nub.

I lick up a few times as she purrs like a little kitten.

My tongue moves down and then back up and suck her clit into my mouth hard.

"Oh God!" Her hands make their way to my hair, holding me to her.

I move my tongue in a circular motion over her clit, sucking and licking fast. I proceed down and lick up her slit. "You are so wet."

"Mmmm…God that's good."

I sink my tongue deep into her pussy, pushing against her 'G' spot, and keep moving up and in and out. I pull out, "My God you taste amazing. I want you to come all over my tongue baby, I need to drink you in."

I move back to her wetness and delve in deep and hard once again. I'm hungry for this woman and need her to come on my tongue.

Her hips buck up and meet my every thrust. "God Buck, that's good. Don't you dare stop. I'm… fucking …I'm coming!" She explodes.

I suck and drink every drop she gives me. I start kissing my way back up to her mouth. "That was incredible."

"You can say that again." She smiles. Her eyes are heavy and so dark. The copper color has turned to a dark caramel color.

"I'm not sure incredible even describes it adequately." I give her another minute, then my hand starts to move south, and my finger starts to penetrate her wet pussy, "Ready for more."

"I want to feel you inside me. I need you right now." Her arms go up to my chest and her fingers begin to play with the hair on my chest and my nipples.

"Oh, we are far from done here. I'm going to see you come so many times, you'll lose track."

I put two fingers in her pussy, moving in and out, massaging her clit with my thumb, and she's almost ready again. This woman is amazing. I massage her clit, finger fuck her, and my lips are on her nipple, sucking hard.

"Buck, please! I need you in me now!" she begs.

I need in her now too. I remove my fingers, pull off her nipple, and hover over her soft body, "You sure you want this?" I nudge her pussy with the head of my dick.

"Yes, please." she begs again.

"Do I need protection?"

"No, I'm clean and I'm on birth control, just fuck me already."

"Oh, my pretty girl wants me to fuck her. Damn, whatever my girl wants she gets." I plunge fast and hard, burying my dick in her wet folds, "Fuck!" *Her pussy is so hot...good God it feels so good.*

"God… yes!" She pulls me closer, so her lips are on mine.

I know she can taste herself on my tongue, and that's a fucking turn-on.

My hips are moving fast and hard, then I slow down, "Is that what you wanted?"

"Yes, God yes… please don't stop." She pleads, her hips meeting my every thrust. "I need you!"

"You ready to come baby?"

"Oh yeah!" she exclaims.

I move my hips in a slightly different direction, start to pound hard and fast, and don't give up. My mouth is on hers, and my tongue trusts in her mouth as quickly as my dick thrusts in her pussy. I find her nipple and pinch and pull it hard.

I feel her pussy walls clench my cock, and her orgasm explodes. I thrust a few more times and follow her over the edge with my orgasm.

"God…that was awesome!" I nearly collapse down on her but catch myself holding up by my forearms.

We are both trying to catch our breath. I'm sweating, she's so gorgeous. What the fuck just happened?

As our breathing slows, I pull out of her and lay beside her, pulling her to me and holding her close to my chest.

"Wow!" She rests her head on my chest.

"Yeah, wow!"

We don't move, we don't talk, we just lie there holding each other, letting the cool air from the air conditioner cool our bodies.

I'm not sure when, but we both fall asleep wrapped in each other's arms.

Chapter Six

Kristie

I blink my eyes and feel a warm body next to mine. What the hell did I do? I slowly move my head and see Buck lying next to me. Oh shit! That's right, I fucked this man. Why did I do that? I never sleep with a man I don't know. God, what was I thinking? I know exactly what I was thinking, I was horny, he was hot, and he was willing. But why this man? He's an ass!

I feel him move and pull me in closer to him. Damn, he feels good, so fucking good. Now, what am I supposed to do? I close my eyes and feel him nudge my neck with his nose, then I feel his dick, hard as steel, against my thigh. Yep, I feel the wetness between my legs, and I want him again. Damn, I never thought I would find myself in this position after our first encounter? How did I get here?

"Good morning, beautiful." His lips kiss my neck, and he nibbles on my earlobe.

Oh, it feels good. "Morning. Is it technically morning if it's still dark outside?"

His hand roams down and finds one of my breasts. "Oh yeah it does."

He pinches my nipple. Yep, I'm in trouble. My pussy starts to pulse with excitement.

"Buck, really… I shouldn't," I tell him.

He looks at me, "Oh yes you should baby. Damn, I want you so bad."

I want him bad as well, but I shouldn't.

His lips find mine, I'm a goner. His kiss is slow, bites my lower lip, delves his tongue into my mouth, and finds mine. His fingertips pinch my nipple, and my pussy is dripping. This man does things to me that no other man ever has. I reach down and stroke his hard cock, moving my hand up and down his shaft. He moans into my mouth.

His tongue starts to move faster, and my hand moves faster on his cock.

I swipe my thumb over the head and smear the pre-cum down his shaft.

Buck pulls back from our kiss, "Damn woman, you are driving me crazy."

I move my hand down and gently cup his balls, "You are driving me crazy too. I'm wetter than I think I've ever been."

His hand moves down my stomach, and his eyes follow his moves. Finding my slit, he moves a finger to my opening, "You are soaked, just for me." He smiles.

My hand squeezes lightly around his massive balls. "Just for you."

He begins to kiss his way down my body, pulling my nipple into his mouth while he plays with the other. He moves farther down, kissing my stomach, licking my skin, and finding my clit with his mouth.

"Oh my!" My body responds to his touch. I lift my hips to meet his mouth.

His tongue moves over my clit, slowly swirling and making me moan like crazy. He sucks it into his mouth, nips it with his teeth, and damn if my pussy doesn't throb.

My hands are on his head, holding him in place, "More…" I breathe out.

He moves his body between my thighs and looks up at me as he literally dives into my pussy with his tongue. His hands are on my hips, pulling me to him. He acts as if he's a starving man and hasn't eaten in a week.

"Buck, God that… shit… so good. Mmmmmm…" I can't think, I can't speak, his tongue is fantastic.

He's watching me, pulls back, "God, you taste good. I can't get enough of this glorious pussy." He goes back to feasting.

I smile. "You are so very good at that."

My hips continue to move up and meet every probe of his tongue. How the hell is he hitting my 'G' spot with his tongue?

"Oh, shit… damn… fffuuuccckkk!" My pussy convulses, and my orgasm is wild.

He drinks my essence and begins to kiss his way back up, licking my clit on his way. He pinches my nipple and nips at it when his lips find mine. I can taste myself on his tongue. He moves his body over mine, placing his hand on the inside of my thigh and pushing it up as he lines his dick up with my entrance.

"You ready for this?" he wiggles his hips a little.

I giggle, "Oh yeah."

He thrusts inside me slowly, moving in and out with precise

moves. His length hits me deep inside, his girth is massive and stretches me beyond what I thought was possible. This massive cowboy is marvelous. I have no idea what I'm doing here. His eyes are on mine, and his body stops moving.

"Hey, where is that mind of yours? I'm doing my best work here and feel like I lost you." Buck interrupts his movements.

I put my hand on his cheek and cup his strong jaw "I'm here. Please don't stop. I need you."

Buck begins to move slowly, kissing my forehead, cheek, and lips. His movements get faster, and he strokes my hair, "You are stunning. Fuck, just stunning."

I pull his mouth back to mine and sink my tongue deep into his mouth as his hips move up and down, his dick moving in and out of my already-soaked pussy. I feel it, I'm coming again.

"Fuck…" my walls clinch, and I explode again.

Buck pulls from our kiss, and his hips stop, "Damn woman, you're driving me nuts. How many times can you come?"

My eyes avert down. "To be honest, this is the first time I've been able to do it more than once."

"Oh baby, we are going to have too much fun. I can't wait to see how many times I can make you come." His lips are on mine again, hard and fast.

Our bodies are moving in sync with each other, and his mouth is all over me, my neck, my lips, my ears, he's amazing. I feel it again, my pussy, damn thing.

He whispers in my ear, "Ready to come with me, baby?"

"Yes." I'm breathless.

His hand reaches between us, his hips move faster, and his dick pounds into my very wet pussy. He pinches my clit, and I lose it.

"I'm coming!" I scream.

64

"Oh… my… God… me too." I feel his dick swell.

I'm thrown over the edge, and he follows me into oblivion.

His body is heavy as he collapses down, then he holds himself up, hovering over me. He kisses my nose, "Damn woman, what have you done to me?"

I smile, "I could ask the same of you."

We lay there staring into each other's eyes for a few minutes when we hear voices outside the office door. His eyes get big, and so do mine.

"Oh shit… I didn't think it was that late." He moves fast, jumping off me and the sofa, finding a blanket that was thrown over his office chair, and tosses it to me.

I use it to cover up and smile over at him, as he scrambles around the room. There's a knock on the door.

"Just a minute!" Buck yells as he pulls on his boxers.

I laugh at him.

"It's not funny. If that's Brock, he's going to give me hell about this."

"So. Is that a problem?"

He smiles, "No, not really." Then he heads to the door and opens it slightly.

"What?" he says gruffly.

I hear a voice, but I'm not sure who it is. Then I hear a few more voices, and Buck says, "I'm busy in here. I'm locking the door. Stay away."

I get up from the sofa and start to find my clothes.

Buck turns around and looks at me, "I'm sorry. I didn't realize what time it was. We get started early around here."

"It's okay. I need to be going anyway." I put on my bra and tank top and pull my shorts on.

Buck comes up to me, "I want to see you, soon. I need to see you."

"Buck, I'm not sure how this is going to work." I point to both of us. "I live two hours away. That's where my work is."

He walks over to me and puts his hands on my arms, "Baby, I know that. I don't want to do anything that will jeopardize your job in any way, but I need you. And I have never needed anyone in my entire life. What can I do?"

I put my hands on his chest, "You turned out to be one of the most amazing men. I don't know the answer to that. This…" I point to the sofa. "… was unexpected, but so good, and I will need to figure it out."

He bends his head to mine, putting his forehead on mine, "I can live with that for now. It's hard for me to get off the ranch, but for you…"

I put my finger on his lips, "I don't know."

He kisses me, softly. His tongue strokes mine, pulls me into his chest, and holds me.

Damn, if this doesn't feel good. But I have to be practical. My job is in Howard County, he's here. This can't work.

"Buck, this has been so much… well… amazing. I can't believe I had sex with someone I just met. I don't normally do that. It was unbelievable and I won't forget it. I just…"

Buck pulls back from me, "Are you kidding me? You're just going to not even try?"

"Buck, I don't see…" I begin to say.

He pulls me into his chest again, and his mouth is on mine fast, hard, and so incredible. How am I supposed to explain this can't work when he's doing that with his fucking tongue. It's like… it's like he was born to use that tongue for all kinds of erotic behavior, and I have the choice of allowing that behavior to continue. Oh shit, I'm in trouble.

I pull away slightly, "Buck, I want you too. But…"

"No buts… we'll figure it out. Just don't give up yet." Buck please.

All I can do is shake my head and agree with him. I want him, and there is no mistake he wants me. But this won't work with us so far apart. I know it in my head.

"Baby, you are one of a kind and we will work this out." Buck strongly says.

I swallow, "Okay, let's see how things go."

"That's all I'm asking." He pulls me close and holds me to his chest.

God, he feels so good. I don't want this to be over, and I'm unable to think when I'm this close to the man. He's intoxicating for sure.

Pulling back slightly, "I need to get going. I'm sure the second body has arrived at my lab, and I need to get over there and get the autopsy completed. Try not to find any more bodies on your property, please."

"But it brings you back to me when there are." He laughs.

I look at him questioningly, "Really?"

He smiles that adorable smile of his, "Just kidding. I don't want any more dead bodies. I do, however, want your very gorgeous, live body here."

"I have your number on the paperwork, I'll let you know when I get back."

"Good, please be careful."

"I will." I pull his head to mine and kiss him one more time. I can't help myself, he's, in a word… incredible.

Buck puts on the rest of his clothes and walks me to my car. Somehow, we miss seeing people when we leave the office, which I find strange. He kisses me one more time, I get in my

Bug and head west out of the ranch. I look in my rearview mirror a few times, and he's still standing there watching me until I can't see him anymore.

What the hell was I thinking having sex with that man? I don't know him. He was an ass when we first met. He's uncouth. He's rude. He's amazing. He's great with his mouth, tongue, and oh that dick of his. Damn girl, what is going on with you?

I shake my head, turn on my music, and try to drown out the thoughts running through my head.

* * *

I'm about an hour out of Howard County when my car starts sputtering, and I pull off to the side of the road. "What the hell is going on now?"

I park, kill the car, and get out. I lift the trunk, and a small amount of smoke comes from the engine. "Great, just fucking great."

I grab my cell from my purse, the paperwork that was in my briefcase and find Buck's number. I begin to dial.

"Hey beautiful, did you already make it home?" he asks.

"No, not yet. My car decided to die on the side of the highway. My parents are in Austin, and you were the only one I could think of to call. I'm not sure what's going on. I'm about an hour outside of Howard County."

"I'm thankful you thought of me, baby. I'll head that way. I'll be there as soon as I can. Try to stay off the road if you can."

"Yeah, there are some trees off to the west of the highway. I'm going to go over there and try to stay out of the sun."

"Good idea. I'm on my way."

"Oh, someone is stopping. Maybe they can give me a lift." I

tell Buck.

"No, don't get in a vehicle with anyone. I'll be there soon."

"Okay, I'll be here." I hang up the phone as a man exits the truck behind me.

"Hey, sorry. I have someone coming to get me." I tell the stranger.

"Lady as pretty as you shouldn't be out like this alone," the stranger creepily says.

I start to get back in my car so that I can lock the doors, "I'll be fine, thanks for stopping."

Chapter Seven

Buck

I hang up the phone with Kristie and step out of my office in the barn. I spot Morgan, "Hey, come go with me."

"Where we headed?" Morgan inquires.

"Kristie called, she's broke down on the side of the road about an hour north of here."

Morgan looks at me, "What'd she call you for?"

I couldn't help but smile, "She needs help."

"I see. What's going on here big brother? You got a lady friend?" Morgan chuckles.

"Shut the fuck up. She's a nice woman."

"Seems to me you two didn't quite hit it off at first. What's been going on?" Morgan teases.

"None of your fucking business. Let's go, the lady's stranded on the side of the road." I grab some jumper cables, my toolbox, and a few other things and throw them in my truck. I'm not sure what is going on with her car, but we may have to have her towed. I let Jack know where we were headed and jump in my truck. Morgan climbs in the passenger side and gives me a great big smile.

I shake my head. "I don't even care."

I start the truck and head out of the ranch. I try to call Kristie's number, but it goes to voicemail. We are heading down the old highway, making our way west and north.

Morgan starts laughing.

"What the fuck's wrong with you?" I ask him.

"I never thought I'd see the womanizing Kyle Buck Stover in love with just one woman. That's all." Morgan keeps laughing.

"I'm not womanizing. That's Brock." I point out.

"Oh man, you have not been Mr. Innocent. You have loved and left so many women, no one can keep up. You didn't stop chasing skirts until after mom and dad died. Admit it, she's special to ya."

Somehow, I think Morgan has realized the one thing that I didn't' want to make public yet. I run my hand down my face.

"I'm not admitting anything. But the good doctor is one special lady." I sigh.

"I knew it. The great Buck Stover is off the market." Morgan laughs again.

"You're worse than Brock, asshole. But yeah, I like her. She's a wonderful lady."

"Damn, she must be really good in bed." Morgan mocks.

"That's enough. I won't have you talking about her like that." I was getting mad.

He laughs harder, "Yep, there it is. You're in love."

I shake my head and turn the radio up, trying to drown out his fucking mouth. About an hour after leaving the ranch, I finally spot her VW Bug sitting on the side of the road with the hazard lights flashing. I pull behind her car, and we get out. Morgan starts pulling stuff out of the back and hauling it to the back of her car.

I walk to the cluster of trees she said she would be waiting at.

"Kristie? We're here!" I call out.

I look around. There's no evidence that she's even been here. I walk back up the embankment to the car, "She's not down there."

Morgan looks at me, "Her phone is in the seat of the car. So is her bag and purse."

I pull my phone out and call 9-1-1, "I'd like to report a missing person. She broke down on the side of the road and now she's gone. Can you send someone out please?"

"Sir, how do you know she's missing?" the dispatcher asks.

"Her phone and belongings are still in the seat of the car. She's not where she said she would be when she called me for help over an hour ago."

"I'll send an officer out. Can you describe the woman?"

I begin giving the dispatcher a description of Kristie and ten minutes later, an officer pulls in behind my truck. "The officer is here, thank you."

"You're welcome, sir," dispatch disconnects.

The officer comes up, "I'm Officer Forehand."

"Kyle Stover and this is my brother Morgan. My girlfriend was here, this is her car. She called me and I got here as soon as I could., but she's not here."

"Have you touched anything?" the officer asks.

I look at Morgan, "I opened the car door and found her things inside. Other than that, no."

I look back at the officer, "She was on the phone with me

when she said someone pulled in behind her. I told her not to get in a vehicle with anyone. She wouldn't have left her things in the car willingly."

"I'll get an investigation team out here. Bear with me." He leaves and goes back to his vehicle.

I look at Morgan, "What the hell is happening? I finally find the woman I want to spend the rest of my life with, and she disappears."

Morgan puts his hand on my shoulder, "We'll find her."

This is not good. Not good at all.

I call JC, "Hey man, you haven't talked to Kristie Smith, have you?"

"No, why?"

"She's missing. Her car broke down, out on the old highway, and she called for me to come help her. When Morgan and I got here she was gone, and her car and all of her things are still here. The highway patrols are here, and they are starting an investigation."

"Oh fuck, that's not good," JC says.

"Where could she be?"

"No idea. Let me make some calls." JC responds.

"Thanks man." I hang up the phone.

What the fuck am I going to do now?

Morgan and I seem to be in the way of the investigation. Officer Forehand comes to me after about an hour, "Mr. Stover, you two go ahead and go home. We'll be in touch. Right now, we've notified her parents, and they are on their way back from Austin. If we have any further questions, we'll contact you."

I head to the truck with Morgan on my heels, "They'll find her man. Hang in there." Morgan reassures.

We get in the truck, and I just sit there for a few minutes, "She's important to me Morgan. Fuck, this is all wrong."

Morgan starts to say something, and my phone rings, "Hello."

"Buck, it's JC. They've found another body, this time closer to the house. It's a man, same M.O. as before."

"What the fuck? I'm on my way." I cannot deal with this right now. My mind is only on finding Kristie.

"Any word on Kristie?"

"No, the police told us to get on back and they'd let us know if they needed us. They've called her parents."

"Shit, that's not good at all. What the hell is happening around here?" JC requests.

"No idea man, no idea."

JC hangs up.

I start the car and tell Morgan, "Another body was found, closer to the house this time."

I head back to the ranch. Cops are everywhere when we pull into the ranch an hour later. JC meets me at the truck, the sun is starting to go down.

"Buck, Morgan. This is getting stranger by the minute. Come on." He gestures in the direction we need to go.

"What do you mean?" Morgan and I follow JC to the house and to my office, which seems to have been turned into investigation central.

JC looks at me, "We've called in the Texas Bureau of Investigations. It's become that serious. The body that was found today, had a note in his pocket."

"What did it say?"

He hands me the note that's been put into a plastic bag.

Mr. Stover,

You really shouldn't be such an asshole. Things seem to be getting bad for you. We know how your ranch is run and how to get to the people you care about. Watch your back.

I look at JC, "What the fuck is this all about?"

"No idea. We need a list of people that have worked on this ranch for the past ten years or so. You do background checks on your workers, right?"

"Yeah, everyone. Pa didn't though. He would hire anyone without question. After he and mom were killed, most of his men left, but Jack and Rooster," admitting to him.

JC hands me a notepad, "Names and phone numbers if you know them."

I look at Morgan, "This is ridiculous."

I go sit in the living room and start to think about Kristie. Does any of this have to do with her disappearance? What the hell have I done? I've gotten the woman I care about, taken. I've put my whole family in jeopardy.

Morgan comes in and sits beside me, "Man, this is not your fault. You have nothing to do with some asshole killing people."

"What if Kristie's disappearance is because of me? What if she's gone because of me?" Questions like this are going through my head over and over and are going to drive me insane.

"Stop it. This family only has room for one psycho and that's me. Let's get that list made and get it to JC," Morgan directs.

I shake my head, "Yeah."

We sit there until dinner time. Morgan calls the rest of the brothers in. We gather in the living room, and Mitch starts, "We need to have someone check on Jewel."

"Fuck! Has anyone tried to call her?" I look around the

room.

Everyone shakes their heads.

"Brock, see if JC can come in here."

Several minutes later, Brock returns with JC following, "What's up?"

"Has anyone checked on Jewel?"

JC looks at me, "Yes, I have a man going after her. They'll fly out of Austin at eight, should be here by ten-thirty or so."

"So, she's okay?"

"Yes, I talked to the man that is picking her up. He checked on her, stayed with her while she packed. She wasn't happy, but she's coming with him."

"Yeah, I don't expect her to be too happy for having to come home in the middle of a semester."

We all seem to find that funny. Our little sister Jewel is a handful. She attends the University of Texas-Austin. She's in her third year as a business major, tough as nails and usually can take care of herself. We seem to have to bail her out of trouble from time to time, but we love her.

Handing JC the list of names the boys and I came up with, about fifteen men on the list have worked here since Pa and Ma were killed. I'm tough, Jack's tough, but we need men that will work. Some just can't hack the work we do. Many people think running a ranch is like on TV—riding horses, playing with cows, and getting the girl. It's not like that. And now my girl is missing, and it could be because I pissed some loser off that couldn't cut it around here.

"JC, any word on Kristie?"

"Not yet, Buck. I'll keep ya posted. Why are you so concerned anyway? Didn't seem you two were getting along very well."

"Let's just say, we worked our issues out. I'm very concerned about her and I'm afraid it's my fault." Worry is all over my face.

"No, it's not your fault," JC says, trying to calm me down.

"I need to find her man, she's… she's important to me."

JC gave me a look, "Really? It's like that, is it?"

I look at him and smile, "Yeah, it's like that."

"I'll keep ya in the loop. We'll find her."

"Thanks JC."

My cell rings, "Yeah?"

"Mr. Stover, this is Officer Forehand."

"Yes sir, did you find her?"

"Not yet sir, but we may have a clue. Did she ever mention a man by the name of Jet Mann?"

"Not to me. Who… wait, Jetson Mann?"

"Yeah, do you know him?" the officer asks.

"He worked on my ranch back several years ago. He was a kid back then. Hot head. How does Kristie know him?"

"We're not sure. He was bragging in the local coffee shop about a pretty young lady that was staying at his house. We are heading over there now to see if we can find him. We'll keep you posted."

"Thank you." I hang up the phone.

"State police have a lead. They'll let me know if it pans out."

Everyone shakes their head.

Rooster shows up at the door. "Buck, I've got food for anyone that's hungry."

"Thanks Rooster. Mitch, let everyone know there's food in here. I need to take a walk."

"Sure thing, need some company?" Mitch asks.

"Nah, I need some time. Thanks." I walk out of the house,

down the stairs, and head to the barn.

This has been the worst day of my life after the best night of my life. I walk to the barn and into my office. I look around, remembering the fantastic night I had with Kristie. Now, she's missing. I can still smell her intoxicating scent. Where could she be? Who is dumping dead bodies on my property? What the hell did I do to piss someone off so much that they want to do this to me? I want my girl back, I don't care about anything else, I want her back, safe and sound.

"Kristie, where the hell are you?" Spinning 'round and 'round the room, running my hands through my hair and feeling helpless.

Chapter Eight

Kristie

I'm so sleepy. Why am I so sleepy? This is the weirdest feeling in the world. It reminds me of the time when my little brother shot me with a tranquilizer dart. I try to open my eyes and nothing, I can't see anything. I'm not even sure if my eyes are open. My whole body feels heavy.

I shake, I hear something but can't see anything. It's so damn dark. I try to blink, and my eyes just won't open.

"He...ll...o? Is...any...one...there?" It feels like I'm whispering.

"Hi," a soft female voice comes from my left.

"Who are you?"

"Emma. Who are you?" she whispers back.

"Kristie. Where are we?"

"I'm not sure," Emma whispers. "I'm not even sure how long I've been here."

"I can't feel my hands. My body is really heavy, and my eyes won't open."

"You have a bandana over your eyes. That's why you can't see. My hands are handcuffed behind me. I'm sure yours are too."

"Who took us?" I ask Emma.

"I don't know. I haven't actually seen any people. Someone comes twice a day to give me food and lets me use a bucket for the bathroom. I have to keep the blindfold on, so I have no idea who they are." Emma starts to whimper a bit.

"Emma don't cry. That will just make it worse. We'll figure this out. How long has it been since they were here last?" I'm a bit concerned, but I need to keep Emma calm.

She sniffles a little, "They brought you in late yesterday. There was another girl that was here when I came in, Stephanie. They came and took her right before they brought you in."

"You don't know anything about them?"

"I know it's a woman that comes in when I go to the bucket. She briefly whispered something to me. I'm not sure about any of the rest. No one speaks. I screamed for so long trying to get someone to tell me what was going on, that my voice got horse and sore. Stephanie said that no one will talk to us."

"Do you know where they took Stephanie?"

"No." Emma gets quiet.

"Okay, tell me about you. Where are you from? How did they get you?" I'm trying to keep her talking, and maybe I can figure out what happened.

"I'm from Dallas. I was leaving my grandmother's out on the Old Highway, and my car broke down. I pulled off and called a tow truck. Before the tow truck got there, this man came up behind me and asked to help. I was standing there with the hood open, showing him where the smoke was coming from, then the next thing I know, I'm waking up here."

"That's right. My car started overheating. I was on the phone with…a friend of mine, when this man got out of a pickup. I was on Old Highway as well." I tell her.

What the hell are these people doing?

I heard a noise, "What was that?"

Emma didn't say a word.

"Emma, what was that?" I ask a little louder.

"Shh…" was all she said.

So, I stop talking.

I feel a nudge on my leg a few minutes later.

"Move." a female voice says. "Pee time," she says it in such a low voice, I almost didn't hear her.

"Where am I?"

"Move," she says again. Then she takes my arm and guides me.

She undid my hands, positioned me, and took my shorts down, pushing me down onto a very uncomfortable bucket. This is what Emma was talking about. God, it stinks so bad over here. This has got to be unsanitary. What must this place look like?

"Ma'am, can I have some tissue?"

"No," denying my request.

"Fine, I'm done."

She pulls me up from the bucket, pulls my shorts up, re-does my hands, and guides me back to where I was. I assume it's a cot because it's low to the ground but not on the floor.

I keep my arms and hands expanding hoping to keep the cuffs a little looser.

"Can you please tell me what you want with me?" I ask.

She pushes me down on the cot, "Stay."

81

"Ma'am? Ma'am…" there was no other answer.

I hear her over by Emma. I can't hear what she says, but I assume it's the same as what she said to me. After a few minutes, I hear a little noise, and then nothing. I am straining to hear anything that might give me a clue, but again there is nothing.

"Emma, are you still there?"

"Uh-hum," she confirms.

"Did I do something wrong?"

"They don't like it when we talk to the woman. A man came in and jerked me by the hair for talking to her."

"Great, that's all I need. We've got to figure out where we are and some way to get out of here."

"There is no way. I've tried to remove my blindfold, but they have it tied so tight, it won't budge."

I start to move my nose, trying to get the blindfold to move. It moves slightly, but nothing is going to make it come down. I feel behind me with my cuffed hands, but nothing. I have an idea. My arms are fairly long, so I try to bunch myself up into a ball and pull my handcuffed hands down under my feet and in front of me, like I have seen on TV before. I am successful and this gives me hope.

Then, I reach up and pull the blindfold down slightly.

As I look around the room, I see there are three cots— mine, Emma's, and one other sitting on the other side of Emma's. There are a few windows around the top of the dark, cinderblock room, but they are too high up to be able to look out. Either it's dark outside, or the windows are blacked out.

The room is small, and I see where the stench is coming from. There is a five-gallon bucket in the corner of the room, and it looks to be about full. That's disgusting.

I look over at Emma, she is smaller than me, maybe five-two or three. She's lying on a very gross cot, but mine's just the same, completely gross.

I whisper, "Emma, is there any way you can bring your arms under you, down under your feet and bring them to your front? I did and was able to pull my blindfold down a little."

Her mousy blonde hair seems very greasy and dirty, her face is smudged with something black, and her face looks like it's bruised.

"Emma, did someone hit you?" Worried that she is really injured.

"No, why?"

"You have a bruise on your cheek."

"You can see me?"

"Yes, I was able to get my hands in front of me and pulled it down. Didn't you hear me?"

"No, I guess I tuned you out or something. I didn't hear anything."

"Emma, try to pull your arms under your feet, so that you can get them in front of you."

I watch as she struggles. She's tiny, but her arms are short, and she cannot get them under her right.

"I can't," she finally lets out.

"It's okay. I'm right here. There are some windows, but they are really high. I don't think we could get up there without something to climb on."

"What do you see?"

"Just a small room, cinderblock walls, three cots, and that piss bucket. I can't see anything else."

Emma begins to whimper again.

"We'll figure it out. I know I have people looking for me.

Surely, they'll find us. Sooner or later, hopefully."

"I have no idea how long I've been here. It could be days or weeks. I don't know. What day is it?"

"It's Sunday, when were you at your grandmother's?" Trying to give her some sense of time.

"Thursday. That means I've been here for three days. No one is looking for me. I was heading home. I live alone. My grandmother is the only one I have left, and she lives out on Old Highway. She wouldn't know I was missing unless she tries to call me."

"Well, I know I have people looking for me. I'm one of the State Medical Examiners, and I was on the phone with my friend."

"That's good. Hopefully, someone will figure out where we are."

"Yeah, hopefully." Buck, I need you, find me. God, please let him find me and soon.

Chapter Nine

Buck

I'm pacing in my office when there's a knock on the door. I open it to JC standing on the steps leading out to the stalls' main room.

"Come on in." I motion for him to enter the office.

"Buck, the state police called me. Kristie wasn't at Jet's place. He had a woman there, but she was there of her own freewill."

"Fuck! Where the hell could she be?"

"Officer Forehand also said that a neighbor had security cameras installed about a week ago. There have been several women gone missing in that area. They are going through the video feeds as we speak," JC informs.

"Oh, thank God. At least they might be able to see what happened."

"Yeah, no guarantees, but yeah. I just got word from my man that went after Jewel, she's a spitfire for sure." He laughs.

I smile, "Yeah, my baby sister is something else."

"Buck?" JC sounds worried about me.

I look up at him. "They'll find her. We just have to give it time."

"I know. Did her parents ever get in?" I ask JC.

"There in route from Dallas now."

"They are more than welcome to come stay here until they find Kristie," I offer.

"I'll let them know. Forehand said that they've been to her apartment, lab, and questioned everyone around. No one has seen her since early yesterday morning."

"She left here around six this morning."

JC looks at me questioningly, "Oh yeah."

"JC, I've known you all my life. You know I don't do relationships. But this woman, she's gotten under my skin. I can't help it."

"It's about fucking time asshole. I wondered when you would settle down and get your head out of your ass. I knew it would take a strong ass woman to put you in your place." JC stares at me with a serious look on his face.

"She sure did, that's for sure. Damn man, we need to find her."

"We will. Hang tough. Is there anything I can do?"

"Not really. I'm not sure what to do myself. What about the body that was found?" This was serious. I needed to know how in the hell these bodies were ending up on my property.

"So far, we have a name for body one and body two. They are running prints on body three, but we have names at least. Body one: Thomas A. Kane, a drifter, originally from Montana. Body two: Arnold Steel, a drunk from Jasper, Wyoming. Body three: Chad White, he was on your employee list."

I look up from staring at the floor, "What the fuck?"

"That makes it personal. And the fact that the body was found a mile from the ranch house, that makes it directed right at you or one of the brothers. Most likely, you." He points at me.

"What the hell did I do to anyone that would cause them to want to murder people and dump their bodies on my property?"

"Men don't want to work these days. They want to be given everything. You are a tough boss, hell, I worked for your Pa back in high school. You're just like him."

I smile, "Yeah, Pa was a mean old bastard, but he was fair. I'm fair, I thought. But if you don't want to work, you won't make it on the Stover Ranch or any other ranch for that matter."

JC put his hand on my shoulder, "Man, we will get this all figured out. It's just going to take time."

"In the meantime, someone is killing men that may or may not have worked on my ranch and dumping their bodies. My girlfriend has gone missing, and God only knows what she's going through right now. What the fuck? I'm not a bad person," letting it all out.

"No, Buck, you are not a bad person. Come on, let's get back up to the house. I need to see if the TSBI have any word on Kristie or the dead men."

I shake my head, "Yeah, I need to know if they found any video with her being taken."

We walk out of the barn and head for the house. When the fuck did my life get so fucking complicated?

JC and I get back to the ranch, and there are cops and men everywhere.

JC shakes the hands of two different men. He looks at me and introduces them, "Buck Stover, meet Mac Terrell and Fred

Norris."

"Nice to meet you both. Any word on Dr. Smith?"

"Not yet, but we are following some leads. I have two of my best people on it, and they are following up some of those leads as we speak."

I just shake my head.

JC asks, "What about the dead men found on the ranch?"

Mac speaks up first, "According to the autopsy of the first man, Kane— his body was injected with a lethal dose of Fentanyl. We've called in Dr. Smith's boss to conduct the other two autopsies."

My chest hurts. It hurts to think she's out there somewhere with someone doing God knows what to her. I put my hand over my heart and slightly rub, trying to get the pain to stop. Mac continues to talk, but I tune him out. All I can think about at the moment is how to find Kristie. What leads did they have? Are they going to pan out? I can't stand it anymore, so I excuse myself and head into the house. Let the cops do their job.

My baby sister stands there when I walk in and pulls me in for a hug.

"Jewel, it's good to see you. I'm sorry you had to come home." I hold her tight.

She knows something is up with me because I'm never emotional. "Buck, what the fuck is going on?"

"I have no idea." I pull away from her and head for the living room.

Our massive living room sits off to the left of the front entryway. It's huge, Pa wanted it that way. There's a fireplace in the front of the room, large, oversized leather furniture, and a wet bar at the back of the room. I head for the wet bar and pour myself a straight bourbon, two fingers, in a shot glass.

"Buck? Talk to me. The boys said this woman means something to you. You never get serious, so what's going on?"

My beautiful sister, Jewel. Her naturally long curly brown hair is piled on top of her head in some silly bun-looking thing, she's wearing a pair of cutoff jeans, a tank top, and her damn boots. She's looking at me with concern in those damn dark brown eyes. Jewel is usually not concerned with anyone or anything but herself. This is a different side to her.

"Baby sister, I don't really know. Yes, she's a nice woman and I...fuck... I don't know. She got under my skin. She's mouthy, stands up for herself, and she's fucking gorgeous. Damn... I have no idea what I'm doing or feeling right now," I admit to her.

She gives me her standard, bigger than life, smile. "You my big brother, are in love."

"What the fuck do you know about love?"

"I'm a woman."

"You're a girl."

Her smile fades, "No, Buck, I'm a woman. You have to get the little girl out of your head. I graduated from high school, I'm in my third year of college, and I've had sex...a lot."

"Oh God, I did not need to hear that." I try to bleach that part out of my brain.

"Well, you need to get your head out of your ass and realize your little sister is grown and can take care of herself."

"Yeah, until you get in trouble and call me to bail you out."

She smiles again, "That's why I love you. Now, this woman. What's her name?"

"Kristie."

"What does she do?"

"She's the M.E. for North Texas."

"Tell me about her," she curiously says.

I shake my head and look down at my boots, "She's…well, she's fantastic. Besides being gorgeous, she's funny, witty, and sexy as hell."

"Brother dear, you are in love. Probably for the first time since Nat," telling me again.

"No, I swore I wouldn't fall in love again. Not after Nat. I can't go through that again."

"But you are. You are standing here, drinking Bourbon, and your heart is breaking. You love her, don't you?"

I pour myself another Bourbon, "I don't know. What I do know is she is missing. She called me to come get her, and I didn't get there in time. She's gone. And…yeah… it fucking hurts."

Jewel comes up behind me, puts her arms around my middle, and squeezes me from behind, "They'll find her, and she'll be back to you soon." She kisses me on the back, "I'm going to shower and get ready for bed. That damn asshole that came and got me, wouldn't give me time to pack."

"You know why you had to come home, right?" I turn around as she starts to head out of the room.

"Yeah, Morgan told me, three bodies. That's a bit concerning for sure."

"It was the note."

"What note?" she demands to know.

"The one that said they could get to anyone I cared about and would destroy me."

"Oh fuck, I didn't know that part. Okay, I messaged all my professors when I got home. They will let me do all my work remotely, except for exams."

"Good, I know this is disruptive." Feeling apologetic that I had to take her away from her life back at school.

"Buck, it's not your fault. Stop apologizing. Hopefully, JC and those cute cops can get all this straightened out soon, and we can all get back to our lives. They will find Kristie."

I look up at her.

"I like her already. I heard she put you and Mitch in your places." She laughs as she heads up the stairs.

I yell up after her, "No, she didn't."

Actually, she did. She was so damn cute when she was yelling at me. Damn, where are you, Kristie?

* * *

I didn't sleep worth a damn last night; I can't keep my mind off Kristie. I can't figure out where she can be, or who's got her.

As I head to the barn, my phone goes off. "Yeah."

"Buck, it's JC, we have a lead, and we think it's where Kristie is."

"Thank God. Where is she?"

"The Feds were brought in on this. Apparently, there's a human trafficking situation going on down by Howard County. They think that somebody took her, and she is in that compound."

"Oh, dear God, I hope she's still there."

"So do I, man. So, do I. They're raiding the compound this afternoon. I just thought you'd want to know."

"What can I do?" I hunt for something I can do.

"Pray brother, pray. I'll keep you posted."

"Thanks man," I hang up the phone with JC and head to the

barn.

Jack and several of the men are getting their horses ready. I look at Jack, "What do we have going on today?"

"We're checking the fence line on the back of the property. Somebody's getting in somewhere to dump bodies. We gotta figure out where they're coming in. I got Little Shit and Mitch working on gates. Checking all the locks on all the gates."

"OK, sounds good. I'm working in the office today."

He nods at me as they all ride out on their horses.

I go back to the office in the barn and sit down to try and do some billing and work. I've got horses coming in, and I've got some cutting horses I need to work on. I've got billing and receivables, but I can't focus. All I can focus on is Kristie and where she is. *How the fuck did I go from just being me, to worrying about a woman I just met a few days ago.*

Chapter Ten

Kristie

Not sure what day it is. Not sure what time it is. Not sure of anything. All I know is I can't see anything. They come around every few hours to see if we need to go to the bathroom. I know there are two of us here. And so far, nobody has tried to do anything to either of us.

I got my hands in front of me, and nobody seems to notice that I'd moved my arms. They're still handcuffed, but at least I can lift my blindfold and look around if I need to. It's not so bad.

Finally, I look over at Emma, and she's trying to get her arms where they're in front of her. "Emma."

"Yeah."

"How are you doing over there?"

"About the same. I'm trying to get my arms in front of me like you did."

"It seems to help, I can at least lift my blindfold. I don't feel totally in the dark."

She's still struggling since her arms aren't as long as mine. "Emma, try to make yourself as small as you possibly can. Bring your knees to your chest. Pull your arms under your butt and up over your feet."

She tries, but it doesn't work. She's getting frustrated.

"Okay, take a deep breath. It's okay. You can do this. This time when you pull your knees into your chest. Push your head down as far as you can, as close to your knees as you can get them."

She tries again, and this time, it works. "I did it!" She didn't yell, but it is louder than a whisper.

"Yes, good girl," I praise.

Emma has to only be about seventeen or eighteen. She's young. I know she's scared, and I don't know what to do except keep her calm.

I lift my blindfold again to see her, "Emma…"

She is looking back at me, "Call me Em. My family and friends call me that, and it would make me feel better."

I smile, "Cool, Em. So, tell me about yourself." I think if we keep talking, it might help.

"Well, I'm a freshman at TCU. I'm a cheerleader and I also play softball."

"That's wonderful. What position do you play?"

"Left field. I have a really good arm and can get the ball from outfield all the way to home plate."

"Wow! That's amazing! I don't think I could throw one from the pitcher's mound."

Em gives a little giggle, "That's funny. I bet with practice…"

Then we hear something. I peek toward the door and tell Emma, "Stay calm."

The one eye that is showing from under her blindfold is big and scared.

It got quiet again, and Emma looks at me, "Put your blindfold back down and stay quiet."

She shakes her head and does what I say.

I watch the door and still don't hear anything. It was quiet, and no one was coming through the door yet.

What are these people doing, and why are we here? I ask myself again.

I don't know how long it has been that Emma and I sit there. It seems like hours since we heard the noise. I think I must have fallen asleep. Then I hear her say something.

"No, please, please don't!" She screams.

"Hello, Emma? What's going on?"

"Kristie, they're taking me. I don't know where they're taking me. Kristie, they're taking me!" she screams again.

"Stop. Where are you taking her? What's wrong?"

Her screams get louder, but farther away. I hear the door slam.

"Emma… Emma… Em, are you there?" I yell.

I wait. I wait for I don't know how long, but I wait. I finally lift the edge of my blindfold, and I was all alone. Emma was gone.

* * *

"Baby, where are you?" Buck says.

"I'm here, I'm right here." I put my hand out and try to touch him, but he's too far away.

"Kristie, where did you go?"

"I'm here, I swear I'm here. Please, help me." I try to get to him.

He's always just out of reach.

BANG! BANG! BANG!

I nearly jump out of my skin. I must have been dreaming.

I hear what sounds like gunshots—a lot of gunshots, semi-automatics to be exact.

TAT…TAT…TAT…TAT… rapid firing, and it's getting closer.

Then dead silence. Nothing, I hear nothing. What the hell? I lift my blindfold. Nothing is around me… God, what is going on?

TAT…TAT…TAT… That was fast and just outside the door.

The door flies open, and a man in a mask says, "Found another one." His mask comes off, and he comes fast toward me.

I recoil back against the wall, "Don't touch me."

"We're here to help. What's your name?" the man asks.

"Kristie, Kristie Smith."

"Found her. She's alive and well. I'm bringing her out."

Who the hell is he talking to? I wonder.

He takes a key and undoes my handcuffs. What? Do all handcuffs have the same lock?

He gently removes my blindfold and pulls me up, "Dr. Smith, we are getting you out of here."

"There was a girl here with me, Emma. I didn't get her last name. I need to find her."

"Ma'am, we are searching for the entire building. If she is here, we'll find her. Can you stand and walk on your own?"

"Yes. We were allowed bathroom breaks, and I walked on my own then."

He assists me up from the cot and makes sure I can stand on my own, "Okay, I need you to stay close to my back as we leave here. Hang on to this loop, and don't let go."

"What's your name?" I inquire.

He smiles, he's kinda cute and seems very young, "Jess, Jess Potter. I'm with the FBI."

I think my eyes grew a few sizes, "Oh…okay. How did you…"

"Ma'am, we need to get out of here. Everything will be explained when we get everyone to safety."

I just nod.

"Now, grab the loop here," he pointed to the back of his vest, "Follow close."

Again, I just nod.

As we inch our way out of the door, he has his gun pointed up and is moving from side to side.

As I look around, there are doors everywhere. It seems like this might have been an old hotel we were in, but it's dirty, smoky, and dingy.

Jess leads me down the long hallway, and we make our way to a door that says stairs. He gently opens the door and checks it before we enter the stairwell. He looks back at me, "You doing okay?"

I just nod.

"Put your hands on my shoulders as we descend the stairs."

Again, with the nodding. I'm too afraid to do anything else.

He keeps his gun up and points, checking around each corner before we go down another flight of stairs. We finally make it to the ground floor, he checks the door, opens it, and leans out, checking for anyone that might be out there.

Before we go out, he looks at me, "Okay, we are going to go to the left. This time, you are going to lead us out the side door."

My eyes get big, "What?"

He whispers, "I'm going to be walking backwards, you will

be at my back walking toward the outside door. This will protect you if someone comes out. I'll have my gun ready."

I form an 'O' with my lips and nod.

As he opens the door, he stands facing to the right. He pulls me out and pushes me behind him.

"Hold onto the loop with one hand and head to that door." He points to the end of the hall.

I grab his loop on the vest and start walking.

Then I hear his gun go off. Damn, that was loud. Something hit the floor down the hall, and I didn't want to look. We don't stop walking, though.

I make it to the door, "We're here."

He says, "Open it slowly, there will be someone out there to get you to safety."

I look up at him, "You're leaving me?"

He smiles, "No, but once you get out to safety, I'm coming back in."

"Okay." I can't believe this is happening to me.

I open the door, and the sun seems to be setting. The door faces the west and is hot and not nearly as bright as it usually is. How long have I been here?

A man comes up to me that is dressed similarly to Jess. He takes my arm, "Are you hurt anywhere?"

"No, I'm fine," I let the man know.

He nods to Jess, and then Jess disappears back into the building.

"Come with me," the man demands.

He has me guarded to his left, and his gun is at the ready but not pointing at anything.

We walk to a building across the street, and he hands me off to another man.

"Ma'am, come with me. We have some paramedics set up over here to take care of you."

"I'm fine. They fed us and gave us water once a day, so I'm not totally malnourished."

"Ma'am, we still need to have you checked out."

"Fine." I walk with him to the opposite end of the building.

There are stretchers set up, and several women are lying on them in far worse shape than I was. Some had cuts, bruises, and dried blood on their faces, arms, and legs. What the hell?

A woman approaches, "Hi, I'm Amanda. I'm a paramedic, and I'll be taking care of you. Please come with me."

I follow Amanda to a stretcher, and she helps me onto it. "Amanda, I'm a doctor. I'm fine."

"Yes Ma'am, but we need to check you out just in case. Dr. Smith, do you know how long you've been here?"

"No. What day is it?"

"Friday."

My eyes bug out, "I've been here for four days? Oh my!"

"Yes ma'am. Please, let me check you over. We need to draw some blood and do some preliminary tests to make sure you are physically fine."

"Yes, fine."

She begins to put the tourniquet on my arm and draw several vials of blood. Then she checks every part of my body. "Dr. Smith, I need to ask, were you sexually assaulted?"

"No! Thank God."

When I said that, someone walked in with a girl in their arms. They laid her down on the stretcher next to me, and I realized it was Emma.

"Emma! Oh my God, you are here."

She looks at me, "Kristie?"

"Yes! Are you okay?" I jump off the stretcher, hug her, and look her over.

She has fresh blood above her left eyebrow, her lip was cut, and she had dried blood on her lip and chin, along with some bruises probably from previous assaults.

"Emma, what happened to you."

A tear rolls down her cheek, and I pull her into my chest and hold onto her.

She cries the entire time they check her out. This is going to take some time to get over.

Chapter Eleven

Buck

JC called me about an hour ago to let me know when the FBI was raiding that awful place, they think Kristie is in. I head to Howard County, so I can be close in case. I don't know if Kristie wants me there, but I can't help myself. I need her, and I don't usually fucking need anyone. I've been a basket case since I found out she was missing. I've yelled at everyone on the ranch, but I'll apologize later. First, I have to find Kristie.

It's been the longest four days of my life. I'm hoping she's there and safe.

I'm almost at the place where JC said the FBI was raiding, and my phone rings. "Yeah."

"Hey man, she's safe and being checked out by the paramedics as we speak." JC's voice is on the other end.

I let out a breath, "Thank God! I'll be there in about ten minutes."

"She's with the paramedics in a secure location. Call me when you get here, and I'll walk you over. Park to the west of the facility."

"Will do, and JC, thanks man."

"No thanks needed," JC hangs up.

I find my way through a small area where JC told me to go on the west side of this old, dilapidated building. I shoot him a text.

ME: JC, I'm here.

JC: On my way.

After a few minutes, I see him exit the west door of what looks like an old apartment building in full tactical gear.

I exit my truck and shake his hand.

"Come on. She's one of the better ones. We've found a mess in that building across the street."

"So, she's safe?" I try to confirm.

"Yes, and she's found a young girl and befriended her."

"I don't care, as long as she's safe."

We walk into the building, down a long hallway, and into a very large room. The windows have been blackened out, there are sheets over several items, and stretchers lined up on both sides of the room.

I scan the room quickly and finally see her. She's holding onto a young lady. I walk up to her, "Kristie?"

As soon as she sees me, she jumps off the stretcher and runs to me, "Oh thank God, Buck!" She grabs me by the shirt and pulls me to her.

I wrap my arms around her and hold her to me tightly. I whisper in her ear, "Thank God you're alright, I was so worried."

She pulls back slightly, "Buck, I was afraid I'd never see you again. Thank goodness you are here. How did you know where I was?"

"JC called me. Are you okay?"

"I am now."

I lean down and take her lips on mine. I've missed this woman and everything about her. Her lips still feel soft, and God, she's so beautiful. My lips briefly touch hers several times, and then I pull back.

"Kristie, have they checked you out? Did they say you were okay to leave?" I ask, making sure nothing happened to the woman I love.

"The paramedic checked me out, but I have to give a statement to the FBI or someone." She looks around the room, "There's someone I want you to meet."

She takes my hand and pulls me over to a young woman sitting on a stretcher. Her hair is a mess, and she has a black eye and dried blood on her lip.

Kristie looks at her and then at me, "This is Emma. We were... uh, roommates, briefly."

"Hello Emma, I'm Buck. It's nice to meet you." I keep my distance. She has a little skittish.

She tries to smile, but her lip won't allow it.

Kristie looks at me, "They had us in the same room together until yesterday. Then they came and got Emma and, well, it wasn't good. They want to talk to the ones that were held longer than me first. According to the FBI liaison, I was the newest one to arrive. Emma has been here for over two weeks."

"How many women have they found?" I wonder.

"Fifteen altogether. Some way worse off than Emma or I. Apparently, they hold you for a few weeks, feed you once a day, let you relieve yourself, then they start the torture. They took

Emma yesterday; she's been in what they called a holding cell and was hit on a few times. She hasn't eaten since yesterday, and she's scared to death."

I pull Kristie to the side, "Babe, when can you get out of here?"

"As soon as I give my statement, but I'm worried about Emma."

"We can take her with us. She can stay at the ranch as long as she needs to. Is there any way you can move your lab? I need you closer."

Kristie looks at me, "I don't know." Then she looks down, "Buck, what are you asking?

"Baby, after the last four days of not knowing where you were, I want you with me, all the time. I know this is super-fast, but damnit woman, I love you."

Her breath hitches, "Buck, seriously? I…I don't know… Oh Buck, I've missed you so much. I know I haven't been the easiest person to deal with, but I don't know. I'm scared. I've got a past you know nothing about."

"Can we talk about this later? I want to know everything about you, and I want you to know everything about me. But I need you at the ranch, with me."

"Emma's family is coming to get her soon. Her grandmother just got the call that she's been found. Can we talk on the way to my apartment?"

I look down at my boots, she's not going to come to the ranch with me. "Yeah, sure."

"Buck, I just need to pick up a few things, then we can head to the ranch."

I look at her with a question in my eyes.

"Yes Buck, I missed you so much. But there is so much we

need to learn about each other, and I have to figure out my job situation. But we can't do that if we aren't together, right? So, I'll come back to the ranch with you. I'll let my boss know I'm taking some time off."

My smile radiates throughout the entire room, "Sounds good to me."

"Now, I'm going to talk to Emma for a few minutes and see if she's interested in coming out to the ranch as well or if she wants to go with her grandmother."

I nod and reluctantly let her go.

I watch her with the young lady, she's very good with people, just not cowboys. Then I smile to myself, well, that's not true either.

I spot JC coming through a door and head this way, "Hey man, thanks for letting me know they found her."

"Buck, this is one of the most messed up things I've ever seen. I've been in law enforcement for twenty years, and I've never seen anything like it."

"Kristie was telling me some of it," I say.

"She'll have to give a statement, then she can leave. We are working on talking to each woman with a counselor present. Some of these women have been here for months."

"I'm just glad that you found them." I let out a sigh of relief.

"Did you know that human trafficking in Texas is at an all-time high? Even on this side of the state." JC is beside himself.

"I had no idea." Shaking my head, not comprehending how someone could do this to another human being.

"Man, keep an eye on Jewel, especially while she's down in Austin."

"She's made it to the ranch. Thanks for sending someone after her. She's a mess, but I'm glad she's home."

"Good, can she finish online or something?" he asks.

"I don't know. I'm going to talk to her about it. She only has until the spring to finish. She's almost done. Her last year will be an internship, and she can come home to do that."

JC shakes his head, "This whole thing has got me upset. I've called Missy six times since we found the women, just to check on her."

"Missy is tough. She could kick ass if she had to."

He laughs, "That's true, but so is Kristie. I'm glad she didn't have to go through what some of those others went through."

"God, me too." I look over at Kristie as she's talking with Emma.

A man and a woman dressed in FBI jackets come up to JC and I, "Detective, we're ready to start questioning the women that can give us a statement."

JC excuses himself and takes them over to Kristie and Emma. Hopefully, we can get out of here once they get those done.

When Kristie started talking, a tear escaped her eyes and rolled down each cheek. I wanted to go to her, but I didn't know if she wanted me to hear what she had to say. I'm not sure what I'm doing. I haven't been in love with someone since just after high school. I never thought I'd find anyone else to love after Natalie. I've dated a few women over the past eleven years, but no one turned me on like Natalie, until Kristie. This woman is a pain in my ass, but God, she's so adorable.

I walk around until they were finished questioning Kristie and Emma. I find some snacks and drinks and grab several, taking them back to the girls. I thought they might be hungry.

JC met me before I got to the girl's stretcher, "They are both ready to go. Emma made a call to her grandmother, and they are meeting her at her apartment. Kristie said that you would be able to take her to her apartment. Is that okay with you?"

"Yeah, I'll do whatever I need to do. Are they ready to leave?" I ask JC.

"Yeah, they've been cleared to leave. You can take them both."

"Thanks man, I'll be in touch. Hey, any word on that investigation from the ranch?"

"We're still processing everything, but I've spent my time the last four days on finding Kristie."

"Thanks man, keep me posted?" I once again ask of JC.

"Will do, be safe."

I walk up to the girls, "I found some snacks for you both. But they said you can get out of here. I can stop somewhere and get you better food." I sit the drinks and food at the end of the stretcher.

Kristie gives me that million-dollar smile, "This is fine Buck, thank you."

"Are you ladies ready?"

Emma looks at Kristie, and then Kristie looks at me.

"I can take Emma to her apartment, no problem."

Kristie moves to me, "Thank you, Buck."

"Let's get you all out of here." I help them down off the stretchers they are sitting on.

I escort the girls out of the dreary makeshift hospital and make our way to the truck. I help Emma into the backseat and Kristie into the front. I make my way around the truck and get in.

"What's your address Emma?" Emma rattles off the address, and I put it into my GPS. She leans her head back on the seat headrest, and I think she's asleep before we get out of the parking lot.

Kristie checks on her a few times, "I'm really worried about her. She went through way more than I did."

"Baby, I'm just glad that you are safe, and I have you back. I know this is moving fast, but to tell you the truth, I don't know what I would do without you now that you are in my life."

I glance over at her, and she was playing with her hands in her lap.

"Kristie, is there something you want to tell me?" I pry.

"Not really, but I need to. I'm not...sure this is the time, however. Can we get back to the ranch and get Emma settled before we have this conversation? I need a shower, and I'd really like to crawl in bed and have you just hold me," she says with desperation in her voice.

"We can do that. No problem. You just let me know when you want to talk. I'll be there."

"Thank you for understanding, Buck."

I reach over and take her hand, kiss the back of it, and hold onto it. We make the drive to Emma's apartment in silence. My girl is tired, and I can tell. She's leaned back, and her eyes are closed.

I pull up to the apartment building, "Emma, Kristie, we are here."

I see an older woman standing outside her car near the apartment building.

Emma gives a big sigh, "Great, my parents."

"Is there a problem?"

"Yeah, they're going to try and get me to go home with them, and I don't want to. My mother is a narcissist, and my dad gives into her every whim. That's why I was staying at my grandmother's."

I look in the rearview mirror, "Emma, you are welcome to come to the ranch and stay as long as you need to. You need to heal, and you don't need stress."

"Thank you, Buck. It's going to be a fight. But that sounds way better than going with them."

I look at Kristie, "Okay, let's get this over with then."

I step out of the truck, walk around and open Kristie's door, then Emma's. As soon as her parents saw her, they run to the truck.

Kristie has a confused look on her face. I look at her with a questioning look, and she just shakes her head.

The mother says, "What took you so long? We've been waiting for hours. They said you were found then didn't know when you would be released. What happened? Where have you been? How…"

"Ma'am, I'm Buck Stover. Emma and Kristie were held together in a room at a place for human trafficking. If we could just make our way into Emma's apartment, she has some things she needs to tell you." I look from the mother to the father.

Her dad nods and motions for everyone to follow him. He apparently has a key because he unlocked the door to apartment 14B. We all walk in, and he closes the door.

Her dad decides to speak up, "Em, I'm not sure who these people are, and I think this is a family matter. So, I think…"

"NO!" Emma yelled, "These are my friends. Kristie stayed with me and kept me calm, until I was taken from the room we were being held in. This is her boyfriend, and they have invited me to come stay at his ranch. I'm going there."

Her mom speaks up, "Oh, I don't think so young lady. You will stay right here where I can keep an eye on you. You are not going anywhere with people we don't know and haven't…"

"Ma'am, Emma, and Kristie have been through a lot in

the past several days. Emma several weeks, and she is over eighteen. I think she should be able to make the decision to go where she chooses."

"Look, Mr. whatever your name is. This is a family matter, and you are not family."

"MOM!"

Kristie must have had enough and decides to speak, "Look everyone, this is no one's decision but Emma's. Neither of you are capable of taking care of her, apparently. She wants to go with us, and she is going to go with us." Kristie turns to Emma, "Come on, we are packing your clothes."

Kristie took Emma's hand and hauls her down the hallway.

Emma's mother starts after her, and I step to the entry of the hallway, not letting her pass.

"Move, you big overgrown cowboy."

"No, I will not. This is Emma's decision, and we will go with what she wants. She's been through hell the past few weeks and needs some time away."

"Do you have any idea what we've been through? No, you don't."

"Yes ma'am, I actually do. Kristie was also taken, and I love her. I know it was only four days, but it was terrifying."

"Yes, that's the word, terrifying," she says. "I was beside myself. No one knew where my baby was, and I had no idea if I would ever see her again. My heart is broken that she doesn't want her family around her. Instead, she wants people she barely knows. How do you think that makes me feel?"

"Frankly lady, I don't care how you feel. My concern is for Kristie and Emma."

She looks at me, then at her husband, "Are you going to just stand there and let him talk to me that way?"

"Look Barb, let her go. She'll come back to us a better person when she gets all this out of her system."

"What? You are nuts. This is my baby girl. I need her." Emma's mother demands.

"No, you don't. Come on, I'll get Mr. Stover's information, and we can check on her when she says it's okay. She's been through enough."

"Well, I never… Where the hell is my husband?" She looks at him as if he is not the man she married.

"I'm right here. But I'm also Emma's dad. If she feels this is what is best for her, then we are going to let her go, for now."

Her dad approaches me, "I'm sorry, we weren't properly introduced. I'm Gary Frost. Thank you for helping out with Emma."

I shake his hand, "She and Kristie seem to have a special bond. I think it might be a good way for her to heal."

"I agree. Her mom is a little possessive." He smirks.

I laugh and don't say a thing.

Emma and Kristie come out of the bedroom with a suitcase. Emma looks like she took a shower, her hair is wet, and she looks clean. The blood that was on her lip is gone. The bruises and cuts are still there, but she seems like she's feeling better.

Kristie comes up to me, "We're ready."

"I'll get this to the truck. Make sure that everything is all locked up."

"We will."

I head to the truck with Emma's parents following me out.

Her mom looks at me and says, "Look, I have no idea who you are. You better take good care of my daughter."

"Ma'am, I'm sure Kristie will be the one taking care of her, but she'll be fine. We have a ranch full of things to do to keep her busy. We have a full-time cook and housekeeper. My sister Jewel is in from college, so there will be another woman around."

A tear slips from Mrs. Frost's eye, "Thank you."

Mr. and Mrs. Frost head off to their car.

Emma and Kristie come out, with Kristie holding onto Emma's arm.

"You ladies hungry? We can stop for food before we head to Kristie's."

Kristie looks at me, "I'd really like to take a shower before we go anywhere, if that's okay."

I take her hand and kiss the back of it, "Anything. I'll do anything for you."

She smiles over at me, and we head to her apartment.

Chapter Twelve

Kristie

I look over at Buck as he drives to my apartment. I wonder how I got here. It feels like so long ago that we had sex, but it was less than a week ago. How do I make a relationship work with my job? It's never worked before, and he lives nearly two hours away.

My mind is going a hundred miles a minute thinking about how I could keep my job and keep this wonderful man that is a pain in my ass.

Buck lets go of my hand, "Oh, I forgot, here's your cell and purse." He pulls my stuff out of the truck's center console and hands it to me.

"Oh my gosh. Thank you so much. What happened to my car?" I start looking through my phone.

"When I found out you were missing, Morgan and I went straight to where they found your car. When we finished up there, Morgan drove the truck home, and I drove your car back."

I laugh out loud, "You drove my little bug? Oh my… How did you fit in it?"

He smiles back at me, "You'll probably have to move the seat, it's moved all the way back. It was interesting for sure."

I look back in the back seat, and Emma is sound asleep. "Shhh…she's asleep." I whisper, "Thank you Buck. For everything."

He takes my hand again, "Kristie, when we get back to the ranch and get you girls settled, I want to talk to you about, us."

"Um…okay. Do I need to be worried?"

"No babe, you don't. Unless you don't feel the same way I do." He gave me that beautiful, dimpled smile.

We make our way to my apartment, and I wake Emma.

As we walk up to the door, I look at Emma. "Emma, while I pack a bag and take a shower, you might want to lie down on my bed and rest for a while. We have a long drive ahead of us."

Emma looks at me with tears, "Thank you so much Kristie. I have no idea what I would have done if I had to put up with my mom right now."

"Happy to help. We are going to get through this together. But you are going to explain to me, at some point, why you didn't tell me you had parents. You led me to believe that you just had your grandmother."

She gives me a smile and nods, "I will. Later though, okay."

"Of course." I reassure her.

We walk into my apartment. "Buck, I'm going to shower and pack a bag while Emma rests."

"Do you want me to run and get some food while you girls get ready?"

"Oh, that would be great. Thank you." I walk up to Buck

and kiss him gently on his lips.

"Anything special you want?" he asks.

"Nothing heavy. We haven't eaten much in the past few days." I give him my house key, so I can lock the door behind him."

He takes the keys, "Gotcha, nothing heavy. I'll be right back." He heads out the door, and I lock it.

I turn to Emma, "Come on, I'll show you to the bedroom. You can rest while I get ready."

"Thank you so much, Kristie, for everything."

"Absolutely, we'll get through this together," reassuring her once again that I will be there for her.

I walk Emma to the guest room and let her lie down. As I move through my apartment, what happened was going through my mind. Five days ago, I had the most incredible sex of my life with Buck. Then, my life was turned upside down. Thank God Buck didn't give up on me. I was afraid I would be a one-night stand.

I never thought I'd have feelings like this again, especially for a damn cowboy. *He better not hurt me... I may kill him if he does.*

I come out of the bathroom, and Buck is in the bedroom, sitting on my bed. I'm glad I had my robe wrapped around me, tied at the waist, or am I?

Buck looks up at me, "Hey gorgeous. How are you feeling?"

"Better, since I got a shower." My hair is up in a towel.

Buck licks his lips and smiles, "Good. Come here beautiful."

I walk over to him, and he wraps his arms around my waist and pulls me close. I put my hands on his shoulders and look into his eyes.

"Kristie, I'm so glad that you are okay. I was scared to..."

I put my finger on his lips to silence him. "I know you were.

I'm just glad that you came to me when they found me. I was afraid…"

"Afraid of…"

"Buck, I was afraid because we had some life altering sex a few days ago, and I thought maybe you…well…that you thought it was just a one-time thing," admitting that I was unsure of what we were, together.

"Not for me. It took all I had to keep from totally pissing JC off from all the texts and calls about where you were. He kept me posted on everything that was going on with the rescue mission. You have no idea how crazy I went knowing I couldn't do anything to help." He pulls me closer, puts his head on my chest, and holds me tight.

"I'm going to be okay. I'm right here. I'm not going anywhere," softly telling him as he leans against me.

"Thank you for agreeing to come stay at the ranch for a while. Have you heard from your boss about your job?" He looks at me again.

"Not yet. If I don't hear from him by Monday, I'll call him again."

"Sounds fair."

"I need to get ready, so we can get out of here." I start to back away.

He tightens his hold and gives me a devilish smile, "Just how good do you feel?"

"Buck, Emma is in the next room. Can't you wait?"

"I can, but I don't want to. But for you, I'll wait for as long as I need to." He moves his hand to the tie on my robe. "Let me help."

"I don't think that you're helping me get ready, will end the way you think it will." I smile at him.

116

"Sweetheart, please. You know I need you. I've missed you so much. I won't do anything you don't want me to do, I promise." He gives me a pouty look, his lip sticking out like a spoiled child.

I put my hands up to his face, cupping his cheeks, "Buck, you know this is a bad idea right now. Emma…"

He stops my thought process when his hands find their way inside my red plush robe and cups my ass. His lips find their way to my nipple, pulling it in and sucking gently at first.

"Oh my…I…ohhh." I let out a breath.

He pinches one nipple hard and nips at the other with his teeth while his free hand squeezes my butt cheek. This man knows how to play me so well already. We just met, but it seems like I've known him all my life.

"Buck, please." I throw my head back, allowing my body to feel his every touch. My brain is on overload, and I'm not sure what I'm doing. My hands move to his head, holding him to me. "Please don't stop."

He switches his mouth and hand, nipping and pinching the opposite nipples. He bites down hard, and the moisture between my thighs grows wetter. I rotate my hips getting as close to him as possible, wanting everything this man is giving me.

Again, he bites down on my nipple, and I lose it. Screaming his name, "Buck! God…yes…I'm…" was all I could get out. I explode and cum runs down my legs.

Buck starts to kiss up my chest, to my neck, "Damn, just from nipple action. That's fucking hot, woman."

He pulls my earlobe into his mouth, gently sucking, as his hand slowly drifts down my torso, finding his way to my clit. "You are so wet, baby."

"Uh, hum, so wet." My thoughts are now not processing. I can't think when this man is in my presence.

His finger finds my clit, flicks it a few times, and I am about to come undone.

He whispers in my ear, "Damn woman, you are fucking amazing."

I feel his finger slide between my dripping folds, going deep and giving a come here movement, hitting my 'G' spot repeatedly. Then a second finger finds its way in.

"Damn…this is…amazing." I explode again.

"Baby, you are amazing," Buck lets out.

Buck removes his fingers, stands, takes me in his arms, and his lips find mine. It's soft, then needy, and passionate. His lips feel so good on mine. His tongue is exploring every part of my mouth.

I can't get enough of his taste, touch, and fantastic sexy body. At some point, he gets me turned around and releases my lips as he gently lies me on the bed. He pushes my robe open, and I'm lying on the bed as I watch this man get undressed.

I smile at him as his shirt is thrown somewhere. I admire his magnificent chest and those damn abs that lead to the perfect 'V' as his jeans are released and fall to the floor.

"Like what you see, sweetheart?" He smiles. You can see the want all over his face.

"Mmmm… Oh yeah, I like." Smiling like a stupid teenage girl.

"God, your body is fantastic. Darlin', I want you so bad."

I scan his body again, and his thick massive dick is bobbing between his legs.

He takes his dick in his hand and begins to rub up and down his shaft.

I lick my lips, "Buck…" It's barely audible.

He moves over me and lifts me slightly, moving me up the bed, then centers himself over me. "You want this?" He nudges his massive cock between my legs.

"Oh yeah, please." I wrap my legs around his waist.

His mouth is on mine as his dick plunges deep inside my pussy. His tongue mimics everything his dick does. I'm already throbbing with desire, wanting to come as he pushes deeper inside. Pulling out, then thrusting in harder and faster.

I moan, "Ohhhh…yeah."

As he continues his thrusts with his dick in my pussy, he looks into my eyes, "You are mine. This pussy is mine. No one else's, do you understand?"

All I can do is shake my head as my ankles clasp around his waist tighter. I feel the walls of my pussy contract, "I'm… coming." I scream his name as my release lets go.

His dick pulls out slightly, the tip just barely in, as he looks into my eyes, "You are mine."

"As long as you understand, you are mine as well. And this dick…" I push my hips up so that his dick goes inside my wetness, "…this dick is mine."

That's all it took, he began to plunge deep, hard, and fast.

I wrap my arms around his neck, tighten my legs around his waist, and hold on for the ride of my life.

Chapter Thirteen

Buck

I kiss her neck, and as I move to her mouth, my tongue finds hers, and my dick moves in and out of her hot wet pussy. God, this woman is absolutely incredible. I can't believe how fucking lucky I am.

"Buck, now…please!" Kristie begs.

"You want this dick baby? It's all yours." I begin to move my hips faster, burying deeper with each thrust. I feel my dick swell inside her as her walls grip my swollen shaft tight.

"God yes…please…I'm coming." Kristie moans out loud.

"Together." I kiss the end of her nose as my orgasm explodes deep inside her, and she follows me over the edge. My God, this woman is astonishing.

I collapse down, holding myself up, hovering over the most incredible woman I've ever known. I look deep into her eyes as she watches my face, and we calm our breathing.

"Buck…"

Chapter Thirteen

I silence her with a kiss— soft, wet, and needy. I don't want to talk; I want to enjoy this for a few minutes longer. I know we need to talk, but I'm afraid of what is coming. She doesn't want me like I want her. It happens, I know it does. This is why I don't date. Women can't stand my lifestyle. Being a rancher is not easy. She's going to say we can't possibly do this because she lives too far. I know that too, I just don't want to face the truth.

My tongue plunges into her mouth, exploring every inch of her. Stroking her tongue, dueling for attention, and I feel myself starting to harden again. My dick loves this woman's pussy. God, I'm in love with her. But how does this work?

Get out of your head Stover. Enjoy the moment.

I pull back and stare deep into her eyes, drinking in her look. She's remarkable, and I can't imagine my life without her.

"Buck, I'm afraid we need to probably get up. I don't want to, but I don't want Emma to think that we are ignoring her if she wakes up."

I smile at her, "Do you know how unbelievable you are?"

She gives me a confused look, "What?"

"Dr. Kristie Smith, M.E., you are the most amazing woman I've ever met."

"Buck, you think that because you just got lucky. Good sex will do that." She giggles.

I push up slightly and look deep into her eyes, "No, I think that because it's true. You are the most marvelous woman I've ever met. You don't take shit from anyone, me included. You help others, you work hard, and you are outstanding in bed."

"Well, you are pretty outstanding yourself. But I'm nothing special. I do what I feel is right and at the end of the day, I can live with myself. You are very special Buck Stover. You, shocked me."

I push up but don't move from hovering, "Shocked you, how?"

"Well, I thought you were an egotistical, self-centered, asshole when I first met you." That smile she gives me, melts me.

"I probably am all those things. I know I come across strong and stubborn sometimes, but when you are around, I just want to throw you down and fuck you senseless," I kiss her nose and move, pulling out of her sweet wetness.

I roll to my side and pull her with me, "Why don't you like cowboys? You told me once that I was egotistical, self-centered, and what was that other thing… Oh yeah, rude. While I can be all of those things, it's mostly toward my ranch hands and my brothers."

Her hand finds my chest and starts making gentle soft circles across it with her small fingertips. Her head is resting in that crook between my arm and chest, and she fits me perfectly.

"Well, I had a boyfriend a few years ago that was a rancher. I fell for him hard and fast. He said all the right words, did all the right things, and moved fast."

"Do you think I'm moving too fast?"

"Maybe, no… I'm not sure. This feels different."

I need to know more, so I ask, "Different how?" I'm softly rubbing her shoulder down her arm and back up again as I listen.

She clears her throat, her hand lying still on my chest as she continues, "Jet was a smooth talking, nice looking, cowboy. He had that Marlboro Cowboy look, ya know. The one that all girls fantasize about."

"Really, women fantasize about a man on a Marlboro

commercial?" He furrows his brows.

"Oh yeah. He's the epidemy of most women's cowboy fantasies." She giggles a little.

"I see, okay. Go on." I need to know more.

"Anyway, Jet, had about a thousand-acre ranch. He ran longhorns mostly. We dated about six months, and he asked me to move in with him. I was shocked, but excited. He was my ideal cowboy."

"I can't believe he waited six months." I kiss the top of her head.

She snuggles up to me a little more, "Yeah, well... He knew I was hesitant because of my family. Anyway, I said yes and moved to his ranch. It was a nice place. He had inherited it from his grandfather. He usually ran about five to six hundred head of longhorns. He had horses and the whole bit. The house was nice, but not as nice as yours. I had been living with him for about a month when he started disappearing every Friday and Saturday night to go into town. He said he had things he needed to do for the ranch. What the hell do you do on a weekend in town that has to do with your ranch?"

"No idea." I keep rubbing her arm and encouraging her to continue.

"Well, it was nothing to do with the ranch directly. He was going across the state line into Oklahoma and gambling."

"Oh, shit... That's not good."

"No, it wasn't. Within a month of me moving in, he lost everything. He came in one night and said that we were going to have to move. When I started questioning him, he got flustered. I had it at that point and just decided to move back to my apartment. I never let it go because I wanted to make sure things were going to work out with him."

"Babe, I'm so sorry. But I don't gamble, I don't chase women. Hell, I barely drink."

"That's good to know," she says.

"Now Brock, he's the woman chaser. Jewel drinks like a fish. And Mitch, he has gambled some, but not a lot. Morgan is to out of it because of the war he was in, that he doesn't want to talk to anyone or go anywhere. You're safe with me babe." I squeeze her close.

She sighs. "Buck, how far can this thing with us go? I live so far away, and I work all the time."

"We'll find a way. You said you were contacting your boss to see what your options were right?"

"Yeah. I'm scared I guess."

"Stop thinking about it right now. We'll figure it all out when we get back to the ranch. Right now, I just want to hold you for a little longer while Emma is still asleep."

She snuggles into me, "That sounds so nice."

We lie there for a while when I hear a noise in the hall. I scoot over and pull my arm from around the now sleeping Kristie, pull on my jeans, and go see what the noise is.

Quietly, I open the door and see Emma standing in the hallway.

"Emma, are you okay?"

"Yeah, sorry to wake you. I just needed a drink of water," she held up a glass.

"If you need anything just let me know. There's food on the table if you're hungry. We'll hit the road to the ranch in a couple of hours. I thought you girls might need some rest."

"Yes, resting is good. I'm not real hungry. I keep waking up though and not being able to sleep well. I keep seeing those…people." A look of fright still in her eyes.

"It's going to take some time to get through all that. We'll help as much as we can."

"Thank you, Buck, you are too kind." She heads back into the bedroom and closes the door.

I return to Kristie's bed and slide back under the covers with her. I pull her back over to me, and damn if she didn't moan. That sound gets my dick hard.

* * *

I must have fallen asleep with Kristie in my arms. I feel her move her hand down my stomach, she's heading for my dick, which is getting harder by the second. I feel her lips on my chest, then my stomach, then…oh my God… "Mmmm… babe…" my eyes flutter open. "Damn, woman."

Her tongue swipes over the head of my cock and fuck me, it's the most sensual thing watching her lick my dick.

"Oh babe, damn…" My hands find their way into her hair.

Kristie's mouth envelopes my dick, and God, it's so warm and wet. She begins to nearly swallow my cock whole. I feel the tip hit the back of her throat as she goes down and back up, working me like a pro.

"God, yes…" My hips start to move up and meet her each time she moves down my shaft.

Her head is bobbing up and down, moving her tongue around the tip when she makes her way back to the end. Then she does it all over again.

"Babe, if you keep that up, I'm going to come." I move with her as she keeps up the pace. "I don't want to come in your mouth, I want to come in your pussy…damn."

She slows her movement, and pulls up, looks at me, "You

don't like this?"

"Oh honey, I love this. But I would prefer to come in you, not your mouth."

She licks up my dick, from base to tip, then moves up my body, kissing and licking her way to my mouth, "How's this?"

She crawls over me, placing my dick at her entrance. "Is this what you want?"

"Mmmm...yes...very much. Are you wet?"

"Oh baby, I'm extremely wet. I woke up wet thinking about you." She looks at me like she is about to tear me apart.

"Good, sit on my dick, babe."

She moves slightly and starts to slide slowly down my shaft. I can't take it anymore and push up into her hard and fast.

"Ohhhh...wow..." she moans.

I love that moan.

Her hips start to move back and forth, then she grabs the headboard and begins to bounce up and down on my dick. Her tits are bouncing, and oh my God, she's incredible.

She throws her head back and starts moving faster.

I grab both her breasts with my hands and start to massage and knead her firm, ample tits between my thumb and fingers.

Her movements become more erratic, and I grab her hips, holding her still, "Just like that baby. Stay just like that."

I pound up into her hard and fast. "Come for me babe. Come all over my hard dick."

She's still holding onto the headboard, her head thrown back, and she screams my name.

That is music to my ears. "I'm coming babe, you with me?"

"Yes...God yes...Buck, please don't stop."

I keep pounding up into her hot wet pussy, and she explodes, growling out her release as my release comes hard. I feel her essence flood my dick and roll down my balls. That feeling is amazing, hot, and oh-so-sexy.

"Oh baby, you are the best. Damn, woman, you amaze me."

Kristie lets go of the headboard and falls on my chest.

I wrap my arms around her and hold her as our breathing returns to normal. I kiss her shoulder and neck and just hold her.

As our breathing slows, she lifts slightly, "That was wonderful."

"You can say that again. We need to take a shower and probably get going."

She shakes her head, "Yeah, you're probably right."

I hold onto her a little longer, and then she starts to move off me. I miss her body already. "Let's take a shower, check on Emma, and get on the road."

"Sounds good." She pauses for a minute, "Thank you Buck."

"For what?"

"For being a great man. For taking care of me and Emma. For coming to get me, just everything."

"Anytime sweetheart, anytime." I kiss her nose. "Now, bathroom…let's go."

She giggles, and we move to the bathroom, shower, and get ready.

We leave the bedroom and find Emma sitting at the table in the kitchen nibbling on the chicken that I had bought hours ago.

Kristie goes to her, "Emma, you okay?"

"I will be," she gives a weak smile.

Kristie stands near her and asks, "Are you ready to head to the ranch?"

"Whenever you two are through canoodling…" She gives us

a shy smile.

We both look at each other and laugh. I look at Emma, "Yeah, we are done, for now." Then I laugh, "I'm going to get the bags in the truck. Let's get going."

Emma stands and pulls Kristie into a hug, "Thank you."

Kristie just smiles, "You ready?"

"Yeah, let's go."

Kristie gathers the trash from the food and takes it out as we leave and start for the ranch.

Chapter Fourteen

Kristie

I see the drive leading to the ranch, and my stomach does flip-flops. I am so excited to be back. I didn't realize how much I missed this place.

We drive down the long driveway, and when the house comes into view, I hear Emma in the back seat, "Holy shit!"

I just smile, knowing she will love it here as much as I do now that Buck wasn't being an ass.

Buck reaches over and takes my hand, pulling it to his lips. He kisses the back of it, smiling, "Welcome home, babe."

"Buck… We discussed this. Well, sort of. We'll see what happens."

He nods, "Yeah, we'll see what happens."

"What is it when you get to this ranch? You turn all Neanderthal on me?"

He burst out laughing. "Neanderthal? No, babe… I want to share my home with the woman I've fallen in love with."

I think my mouth must have hit the floorboard of the truck when he said that and in front of Emma, too. Men pick the strangest times to tell you they love you.

His smile fades a bit. "I know I'm an ass and I know I don't do the right things all the time, but I do know for a fact I love you."

He stops the truck in front of the house.

Emma opens her door. "I'll just leave you two alone for a minute." She gets out of the truck, closes the door, and I watch her walk up the steps and sit down on one of the chairs sitting to the left of the front door.

I look over at Buck, "You're timing sucks!"

"Yeah, I'll work on that." He's smiling from ear to ear.

"Buck, my feelings for you are...wow...Buck, I do love you."

He nearly hurdles the console of the truck and attacks my mouth. He grabs my face with both hands, and his lips are on mine faster than a rabbit runs from its prey.

I place my hands on his, and all I could do is smile as he tries to kiss me.

His lips begin to move over my face, reaching my earlobe, and he sucks it into his mouth, causing me to moan.

"I love that moan, I want to hear it all the time. Can you please do everything you can to be here with me, perma-nently?"

"I'll do my best. But I love my job, and I will not quit."

"I know, and I never want you to do anything you don't want to do. But I need you, and I need you with me all the time. I need to make love to you as much as humanly possible."

His lips find mine again. This time, he slowly nips at my lips, swiping his tongue across the seam, and I open for him.

I love everything about this man. His taste, his smell, his...

yeah…his dick…everything. He is amazing.

After a few minutes, I pull back slightly. "Babe, we need to see to Emma. She's still sitting on the porch trying to… Oh shit, Brock just stepped out of the house." I reach for the truck's door handle, and Buck stops me.

"Wait, let's see what happens."

"Oh no, I'm not going to let Emma be another notch on your brother's bedpost."

He laughs, "Good point."

Buck got out of the truck, "Brock, leave her alone."

Brock's face is priceless.

His eyes bug out, his mouth drops, and he looks like he is starting to sweat. I had to smile.

Buck looks at me, then back at Brock, "Leave Emma alone."

"Buck, I was just introdu…"

Buck stops him, "I know exactly what you were up to."

"Oh Buck, seriously," Brock starts again.

Buck took Brock by the collar and hauls him toward the barn. He yells back at me, "I'll be right back, babe."

I laugh as I walk up the steps.

Emma looks at me, "What was that all about?"

I shake my head, still smiling, "Brock is something else."

"He seems nice." She shrugs.

"He is, but he is also a player," warning her about Brock's extra-curricular activities.

"Oh… I see." Emma stands from the chair she is sitting in.

"Come on, we can wait inside where it's cooler."

Emma follows me into the house.

As we enter, a dark-haired woman is sitting on the sofa. *She is gorgeous*. Her long chestnut hair is curly and falls down her back, all the way to her waist. Her smile is big and infectious.

Her light brown eyes sparkle as she smiles.

She looks at us as we walked in, "Well, hello you two. You must be Kristie and Emma. Buck called ahead and told us you were coming. I'm Jewel, the only girl of the family. I'm so glad to see you both. Women around here are rare." Jewel stands and approaches us, pulling me in for a hug, and then Emma.

Emma is taken aback a bit by the girl's forwardness.

I laugh, "Good to finally meet you, Jewel. I'm Kristie."

"So, you're the one that finally settled my big brother down. Damn girl, you must have the best pussy in Texas."

I think my mouth must have dropped to the floor again, "Um…"

She starts laughing, "Come on, I'll show you to your rooms. Kristie, you'll be in with Buck, of course. And Emma, you will be across the hall from me. If you need anything at all, just knock on my door. I'll be heading back to college as soon as Buck releases me from my prison."

I start, "Jewel, someone is trying to get to Buck or someone on this ranch? Didn't the guys fill you in on what's been going on?"

"Oh yeah, but good lord, I'm in Austin, no one will get me there. I need to get back, I have… Well, let's just say I'm a busy girl." She points to a closed door, "That's Buck's room there and Emma, this is your room." She points to another closed door a little way down the hall. "You girls get settled in. Rooster has a meal fit for a king, or queen, ready for tonight."

Emma looks at her, "Rooster?"

"He's the cook. I was sure you met him already."

I look at her, "I've heard his name. Thanks Jewel, for showing us to our rooms."

"No problem, see ya both at dinner." Jewel smiles and moves

down the stairs slowly.

I glance at Emma and mouth *'wow'* and then we both laugh. "Do you need some help unpacking?"

Emma smiles, "No, I didn't bring that much."

"Okay, I'll go put my stuff up and meet you back downstairs in a few minutes." I turn to open the bedroom door.

"Hey Kristie…" Emma's words stop me.

I turn back, "Yes?"

"Thank you."

"Oh Emma, thank you. First of all, you saved me. Second, I'll do anything for you, and third, we have to stick together."

She smiles and moves to the bedroom Jewel indicated was for her, then she disappears into the room.

I open Buck's door and about hit the floor. It was the cleanest men's bedroom I've ever seen. His bed was even made.

The bedroom is large, and it looks like it was the master bedroom. A large, oversized log bed is in the middle of the room. The bedding was masculine, with tans, browns, and taupe's. There are side tables with drawers on each side of the bed, lamps in the middle of each, and clean as a whistle. At the far end of the room is a wardrobe, beautifully handcrafted, double doors with some intricate design on each door.

To the left of the bed is a door, and I open it to see what it is, the closet or bathroom. It is the largest walk-in closet I've ever seen. I switch the light on. Shirts, jeans, and colors organized, and the boots were arranged along the back wall. I don't think I'd ever seen this many boots anywhere but a shoe store.

To the right of the bed is another door, I assume the ensuite. I walk around the bed and open the door. As I walk in, there is a long double vanity to the left, stained in a pinewood color to match the bedroom. There are cabinets on each side of the tall mirrors and under the sinks that spread over nearly the entire wall. At the end of the vanity is another door, opening it, there is the toilet. "Well, that's interesting." Across from the vanity is a large soaker jetted tub. "That looks like it would hold three or four people, damn."

On the right of the door is a large walk-in shower. Large glass blocks surround it, and the tile is a beautiful ceramic with a combination of colors in the neutral range. The bathroom is almost as big as my apartment. It is huge.

I walk back into the bedroom, and Buck walks in. "Hey baby, are you finding your way around okay?"

"Buck, this is the nicest bedroom I've ever seen. And that bathroom…is amazing."

Buck smiles at me, "I think you're going to like it here." He walks over to me and pulls me into his arms.

I wrap my arms around his neck, "Buck, I love it here, but I still have a job."

"I know, it will all work itself out." His lips were on mine in a soft, slow, demanding kiss.

After a few minutes of his luscious kisses, I pull back and smile at him, "How did things go with Brock?"

He smiles back at me, "There will be no issues with my little brother and Emma. I made sure of that."

I step back a little, "Buck, what did you do?"

"I just made sure that he knew, as well as every other man on this ranch within a shouting distance, that Emma is off limits to any man."

"Oh Buck, what if she finds one of them to her liking? She might find her a cowboy like I did."

"Well, it won't be Brock." He laughs. "He was taken by her though."

Chapter Fourteen

I pull out of his arms, "Where would you like for me to put my things while I'm here?"

"Baby, you can use anything that's mine. Clean out drawers, take up my closet, my place is yours." He tries to grab my arm as I walk to the other side of the bed.

"I need to unpack. Your sister…"

"Oh, you've already met Jewel?" he asks.

"Um…yes…she was in the living room when we came in. Apparently, Rooster is making a meal fit for a king, or queen."

"Hmmm…okay. Rooster always fixes a meal fit for a king. Make yourself at home, my home is yours."

I look at him, "Buck, do you think we are going a little fast?"

"Not at all. I think…" He walks toward me. "… We are going just fast enough for us. If we need to slow down, you tell me. But I think we are doing just fine. I know I love you and when you were missing, all I could think about was getting you back."

"I have a confession to make. When I was in that room, all I could think about was you coming to rescue me. I wanted to see you more than anything."

He takes me in his arms, "Baby, I will always come for you." He leans down and kisses me. His lips are soft, his tongue delves into my mouth, and we have the most passionate kiss I think I've ever had.

He pulls me closer, and I can feel his erection through his jeans. He puts his hand under my shirt, and his cell goes off.

I pull back, "Saved by the bell."

"That's not funny. I was really getting into that. I wanted…" His phone rings again. "Damn it."

He pulls his cell from his pocket, "Buck, this better be good."

I start to look through the closet while he's on the phone. I hear him say, "Yeah, okay, sure thing, see ya soon.

He hangs up the phone, "That was JC. He's heading out here in a little bit. He thinks he has a lead on who is putting dead bodies all over our property."

"Oh…that's great. I hope they catch whoever it is. This is getting a little serious around here."

"Yeah, he'll be here around dinner. So, hopefully we will find out what's going on."

"I'll just finish unpacking and then I can head downstairs and help if I need to."

"Baby, we have people to take care of everything around here. I do want you in with JC when he tells us what he's found."

"I can do that. What about Emma?" I wonder.

"I'll see if Jewel can take her for a walk and show her around the property."

"That's a great idea."

"I'm going to go check on some things in the barn. If I stay any longer, I'll have you in that big bed and having my way with you."

I smile, "Well…as much fun as that sounds, let's keep it for later when we don't have a detective coming for dinner."

He laughs, "Yeah." He pulls me into him and gives me a soft kiss. "See you in a little bit."

"Okay." I watch him walk out the door.

Damn, that is one fine man. I need to figure out how this is all going to work.

I'm hoping JC has some news we can use and figure out who is dumping bodies on the ranch.

Chapter Fifteen

Buck

J ewel is sitting in the living room, on her laptop, as I walk down the stairs.

"Hey sis, whatcha doin'?"

"Working on a class. What are you doing?"

"I'm heading out to the barn. But I have a favor to ask." I look at her with a straight face.

She gives me a go-to-hell look, "I'm here. Other than that, no more favors big brother."

"Jewel, you know we are trying to keep you safe." Again, with the look.

"I'm perfectly fine in Austin. I have my bodyguard and I know…" There was a scream from upstairs.

We both jump and bolt to the stairs.

When we reach the top of the stairs, Kristie runs to Emma's room.

"What's going on?" I ask, out of breath from running up the

stairs,

Kristie looks at me, "No idea. Emma screamed, and I came running out of the bathroom."

Kristie opens the door, and Emma is sitting in the corner, on the floor, shaking. Kristie approaches her slowly. "Em? It's Kristie. What's going on?"

Emma looks like a frightened kitten staring at Kristie. I couldn't hear what Kristie was saying to her, but Emma's eyes were bugging out. She was sweating and shaking like a leaf.

Jewel looks at me, "Buck, can you get her a bottle of water from the kitchen?"

"Yeah, be right back." I run down the stairs into the kitchen, grab a bottle of water from the fridge, and was back upstairs in less than a minute. I hand it to Jewel, and she takes it to Kristie.

Kristie takes the bottle, opens the lid, and hands it to Emma.

Emma is starting to come around and asks, "What happened?"

"You screamed, and we all came running," Kristie tells her with that kindness that I love about her.

"Oh my gosh, I'm so sorry. I don't know what happened." Emma looks at us in confusion.

Kristie helps her stand, "What were you doing before you screamed?"

"The last thing I remember, I was lying down on the bed. I must have fallen asleep. I'm so sorry."

"No need to be sorry," Kristie reassures her.

Emma looks around the room and notices that Jewel and I were there. Jewel walks over to her, "Hey, would you be interested in taking a walk with me later? I'd like to show you around. That might get your mind off…things."

Emma shakes her head, "I think…I might need a shower."

Kristie has her arm around Emma's shoulders, "That will probably help you feel better. Was it a bad dream?"

"I don't remember. All I remember is lying down, then you guys came in." Emma shakes her head. "I can't remember what was going on in between."

Jewel looks at her, "Let's get you in the shower. A nice long hot shower will do some good. Then we can go for that walk after dinner. Do you ride horses?"

Jewel and Emma are about the same age. Jewel is this high-spirited tomboy, and Emma is a fragile-looking girl. I'm hoping Jewel can help her while she's here.

Jewel and Emma disappear into the bathroom just outside the bedroom in the hallway. I look at Kristie, "I wonder what that was about?"

"I don't know. She hasn't talked to me about what happened when she left our room at the compound. I wonder what they did to her."

"She may need some counseling. It might help her," giving my opinion about Emma's situation.

"I'll talk to her tomorrow about that and see what she thinks."

Buck pulls me into his side, "I'm going to check on dinner. JC should be here pretty soon."

"Okay, I'm going to go get ready for dinner." Kristie stands on her tiptoes and kisses me.

"Hey, I love you."

"Hey, I know you do. And I love you."

I think my face may break from all the smiling. This woman is something else, and I can't stay away from her. I watch as she walks back into my bedroom. That's where I want her all the time. She's mine, and I don't want to lose her.

I walk down the stairs, and JC walks in the door. I shake his hand, "Hey man, thanks for coming out."

"Not a problem. We have a couple of leads, and I'm hoping one of them will pan out. We'll talk later though."

"Sounds good. The girls will be down in a bit for dinner, let's have a drink."

We walk into the living room, and two of my brothers are already there, Mitch and Morgan. They have a drink in each of their hands.

Mitch looks at us, "Hey JC…Buck. Want a drink?"

"Yep, sure do," we both answer at the same time.

We all laugh for a minute.

Mitch goes to the bar, "I'll get ya one."

"Thanks," I say.

Morgan looks at JC, "So, what's the news?"

JC looks at us all, "I'll go over everything after dinner. I don't want the girls to come in unexpectantly."

Morgan nods in agreement.

About that time, we hear female voices.

All three beautiful women walk into the living room laughing and smiling, even Emma.

Jewel is really good with her. I'm hoping she can get her to open up.

"Ladies." I walk over to Kristie and kiss her forehead as I pull her into me.

JC's eyebrows raise, and a smile spreads across his face, "I'm going to guess you two are an item."

Kristie smiles, "Yes we are, thank you very much."

Mitch is still standing over by the bar.

Kristie looks at him, "Are you playing bartender tonight?"

"I guess so, what can I getcha?"

She smiles at him, "Do you have white wine?"

"I think so. Um… We haven't been formally introduced to this lovely lady," Mitch starts toward Emma, smiling.

I stand between him and Emma, "Mitch, Emma. Emma, Mitch. And that one over there is my other brother, Morgan. Now everyone is introduced. What I told Brock earlier, goes for the rest of you assholes."

Mitch threw his hands up in the air, "I was just going to be polite." He turns to Emma, "What can I get you to drink beautiful?"

I think Emma blushes slightly, "I'll just take a Coke if you have one. I don't usually drink."

"I'll get ya one. We have several different kinds of soda."

"Thank you." Emma seems withdrawn, and I'm unsure how to get her out of it.

I look at Kristie and whisper, "She okay?"

"She will be," she nods and whispers back.

Brock comes into the room about the same time Mitch hands Emma her Coke.

"Thank you…um…"

Brock spoke up, "That's the other asshole, Mitch. Buck being the first asshole."

"What's your problem tonight, little brother?" I ask as politely as I can. What I want to do is kick his sorry-mouthing ass all the way back to the bunkhouse.

"Nothin' much *big brother*. Just keeping to myself," Brock says, rolling his eyes at Buck.

Emma sits on the sofa next to Jewel, and they are whispering about something.

I shake my head as Brock goes to the bar and fixes himself a drink. I am about to say something more, but Rooster comes in and announces that dinner is ready.

"My lady, are you ready?" I stand by Kristie, take her hand, and pull her to me.

She smiles, "It smells delicious."

"Rooster has to be the best cook this side of the Mississippi."

We all make our way into the dining room.

Rooster has set the table with the dark brown and teal stoneware, the good silver, and it's decked out with napkins in the glasses and everything. He really went all out.

Kristie leans into me, "Does it always look like this? I don't remember seeing it like this before."

"No, Rooster is trying to impress the ladies tonight." I kiss her forehead and pull her chair out for her.

I notice that Brock has pulled Emma's chair out for her and sits next to her. I am giving him the stink-eye from hell. The damn fool just smiles at me and starts talking to Emma.

Morgan pulls Jewel's chair out for her. Our parents made us use our manners when women were around. I can't remember a time when Pa didn't pull Ma's seat out for her when we had dinner.

Pa was a tough old bird but had a gentleman's heart.

We sit down to a fine meal of ribeye steaks, baked potatoes, salad, and garlic green beans. Garlic bread and butter are sitting in several places on the table.

The glasses are filled with sweet tea, and the conversation stays light as we all dig in.

Once dinner is over, the men head to the living room with Kristie following me. Jewel and Emma disappear out the front door.

JC stands near the large fireplace, and the rest of us take seats around the room. Kristie sits near me on the large, oversized chair.

I look at JC, "You're up."

JC takes a deep breath, "We've found a few links to a person that worked on the ranch back in the day when your Pa was still alive. We've been looking for Buster Elliott. Does that name ring a bell with anyone?"

I look at Morgan, "You remember him don't you. He tried to beat the shit out of ya when you were five."

"Holy shit, that guy was an asshole and meaner than hell."

I look at JC, "Elliott was a mean old cuss. He had to be in his fifties when he worked here. Pa hired him on because he was sitting at the diner complaining about needing work. His old lady left him for a younger man, so he was a sour old man."

JC looks at me, "That would put him around seventy something now. That can't be him then. Damn…"

"What about a son or relative of his that he has doing his bidding?" Morgan asks.

"Maybe, but we haven't found any of his family. Like ya said, the wife was out of the picture. I'll do some more digging. But the reason we think it might be him is because we found a partial print on the last victim that matched Buster Elliott. His prints were on file due to several drunken disorderly charges back when he was younger."

Kristie looks around the room at all of us. "What did the autopsy say about the last victim? I didn't get to do that one. Was he killed like the other two?"

JC shakes his head, "Yes, lethal injection of fentanyl."

"So, it has to be someone that can get their hands on the drug," Kristie says.

"Fentanyl seems to be making rounds in the illegal sector. We have more OD's on fentanyl than any other drug right now.

The FBI are working on these leads. This is just all I know so far."

The front door slams open, and one of the ranch hands, Jim Nelson, runs in. "Buck, you have to come quick. The girls found another body."

I look at JC, "Call your buddies in." Then I look at Kristie, "I guess you are back at work."

"I'll go get my kit out of the bedroom. I never leave home without it. I'll meet you at the barn." Kristie heads upstairs.

JC looks at Jim, "Where was this one found?"

"At the back of the barn, in a blind spot for the cameras."

"Holy shit, this is getting way too close. How the hell did they get that close, and no one see them?" I'm furious.

We all head down to the barn. Jewel and Emma are coming back to the house.

Jewel looks at me, "He's in the back corral."

"Is she okay?"

Jewel just nods.

I nod and head that way.

By the time we all get there, all my ranch hands are standing around outside the corral.

The bunkhouse is just a hundred feet away from the back corral. How the hell did no one hear anything?

JC has his phone to his ear, "We need the crime lab here ASAP," he says then hangs up.

Kristie puts on her gloves and heads to the body. She takes pictures of the crime scene and the body from several angles and proceeds to start her job. I watch in amazement. She's precise, very professional, and so fucking adorable.

JC steps next to me, "The crime lab is on the way. I've called in the FBI, and we are going to need a copy of all the video footage you have around the barn."

I look over at Mitch, "Get the video feeds."

Mitch heads for my office in the barn where all the video equipment is.

I look over at Kristie, and she is rolling the body over on his back, and gasps.

Chapter Sixteen

Kristie

What the hell have I walked into? Who is killing these people and dumping them on the ranch? I hope JC and his team can figure this out soon.

The body is face down in the dirt. He has a pair of baggy jeans, a denim jacket, and a hat. When I roll the body over, I'm in shock.

"Oh shit!" It's a woman. Who the hell did this?

I continue my investigation of the body, checking under her nails, hair, around the body, and clothing. This is ridiculous, and I have no idea why anyone would do this to a woman, or anyone for that matter.

I stand from where I've squatted near the body and look up at Buck. His face is distraught, and he looks lost.

I gather my supplies, making sure all the evidence bags are labeled correctly and put them in my case. I remove my gloves, place them in the case, and then make my way over to Buck.

I put my hand on Buck's forearm. He's standing like a statue with his arms crossed over his massive chest. His face is sullen and broken. "Buck, this is not your fault. They'll figure out who is doing this, and things will return to normal."

"Will they? Someone is planting dead bodies on my property. This is personal. It's got to be about me." He's nearly yelling at me. Then he turns and storms off.

Mitch comes up to me, "Let him cool off a bit and he'll be fine. This has him rattled for sure!"

I shake my head and walk over to JC. "What can I do?"

"Kristie, I really don't know. The FBI is on their way. The lead I had didn't pan out. The other lead, I didn't get to talk to Buck about before this body showed up."

"Mitch said to let him cool down a bit, and then he'll talk to you."

"This is body number four and it's a woman, that's some messed up shit." JC turns and walks away.

I stand watching as the wagon loads the body. I'm not ready to leave, but someone has to do the autopsy. I pull my phone out of my back pocket and hit my boss's number.

"Dr. Leonard, it's Kristie Smith. I'm at the Stover Ranch, and there's been another body found. A woman this time. Who did the last autopsy?"

"I did, Dr. Smith. I wanted to make sure it was done to your satisfaction. I'll email you the report. Do you want to do the autopsy on the new body, or do you want me to do it?"

I look down at the ground and shuffle my feet against the dry earth, contemplating what I should do. I need to stay with Buck and make sure he's okay. I want to go and do the autopsy. Shit!

"Dr. Smith, I can have the lab in Big Springs open up for you.

Would that help?"

"Oh, yes sir. That would help. It's only about thirty minutes from the ranch. Thank you."

"I'll make the call and get you there. Let the driver of the bus know to take the Jane Doe to Big Springs."

"I'll do that." I take off toward the van that just put the body in the back. "Thank you, Dr. Leonard."

"You are welcome. I hope they find out who is doing this."

"Me too sir, me too." I hang up the phone and walk up to the driver of the autopsy bus. "Could you take the body to Big Springs? My boss is making the arrangements."

"Yes, ma'am," the driver says.

He gets in the driver's seat, and then heads back down the drive.

I go in search of Buck to check on him.

* * *

I find Buck in his office in the barn. He has his face in his hands and elbows on the desk.

I clear my throat to get his attention.

As he looks at me, his eyes are sullen and lost still. I walk over to him, put my hands on his face, and pull him into me. His arms wrap around my waist, and he buries his face in my stomach. I hold him and let him process what's happening.

He loosens his hold on me, looks at me, and says, "What the hell is going on?"

"I don't know sweetheart. Hopefully the FBI can figure it out. JC said they have another lead he didn't get to tell us about, but not sure if it will pan out."

"This is so close. Who are these people? I haven't recognized anyone of the dead bodies. I can't figure out why anyone would kill someone and leave them on my ranch."

"Could it be someone that worked for your father?"

"I don't know, maybe."

I sit on his lap and wrap my arms around his neck. "Buck, I have no idea what's going on. We just need to leave it to the authorities. They'll find who is doing it."

When he looks at me, my heart melts. His eyes are sad pools of light blue staring at me. There is so much emotion in his eyes. He feels for those people that have been killed and dumped here on his ranch. You can see it in his eyes, all the way to his soul.

Buck moves his hand to the back of my neck, cradling my head in his hand and rubbing soft, gentle strokes across my cheek with his thumb. "What did I do to deserve you?"

I smile at him, "You were just your stubborn self."

He laughs, "That I was. And I was up against a strong headed woman."

He pulls my head down, placing his lips softly on mine. He nips and bites at my bottom lip.

I open my mouth and devour his. Maybe if I drown out his thoughts on the murders, it will help him.

Buck begins to rise from the chair and cradles me in his arms as he lifts me. He moves us to the sofa. *The* sofa. The one that I found out just how wonderful this man can be. He lies down on the sofa pulling me on top of him.

I can feel his erection against my stomach. I move so that I am now straddling him. I pull back from the kiss and stare into his eyes. I watch as this gorgeous man watches me.

I sit up, with one leg on either side of his body, and pull my top over my head. I can feel my nipples harden and my pussy throb. This man does that to me every time.

The buttons on his shirt become bothersome, and I rip open his shirt, buttons flying everywhere.

"Damn woman, you in a hurry?" He smiles.

"Yes, yes I am sir. I needed to get to this massive chest of yours." I begin to rub my hands up and down his torso. I can't get enough of him.

My hips are moving back and forth over his already hard dick, and my pussy needs a release and fast. I move my hands down, undo his belt buckle, unbutton his jeans, and let the zipper down. My hand finds its way into his jeans and under his boxers.

"Oh my God, Buck. You are so fucking hard," I moan in a gravelly voice.

"You do that to me. I get hard just thinking about you."

I smile at him and scoot down a little, looping my fingers in his jeans and pulling them down. His boxers are next, and his nice large dick is jutting out, just begging for me to lick it.

Moving down a little more, I lean down and put my mouth on his hot hard dick. Licking up the shaft, I twirl my tongue on the head and lick off the pre-cum before sliding my mouth down the length of his shaft.

He moans loudly. "God babe, that's good…mmm…fuck…"

I continue moving my mouth up and down his cock, bobbing my head, making sure he is satisfied.

"Kristie, if you don't stop now, it will be too late, fuck…" he groans.

After a few more strokes in and out of my mouth, I need to be riding this man. I stand, remove my shorts, panties, and bra and climb back on top of him. I center myself over his dick, putting the tip right at my opening. "You want this?"

I rub his dick into my lips, letting him feel how wet I am.

"Baby, if you don't sit down on my dick right now, I'm turning you over and plunging in."

"Damn…" I smile, as I slowly allow his dick to slide into my pussy.

"Fuucckk!!" he loudly says.

I smile again and begin to move my hips. "Is that what you wanted?"

"Damn straight."

I start to bounce, my boobs are bobbing up and down, and he grabs them both with his hands, squeezing the nipples and pulling me down so that he can take one of them into his mouth while he pinches the other nipple between his thumb and finger.

He sucks, nips, bites, and sucks some more on my hard nipples.

"Oh damn…I'm…coming," I keep bouncing harder and faster on his dick.

He grabs my hips, stills me, and pistons up into me harder and faster than I was moving. He moans as he watches my boobs bounce uncontrollably.

"Fuck…damn…shit…" I grab the back of the sofa and brace myself with the other hand on his chest.

He keeps moving in and out, faster, and faster.

I throw my head back, screaming his name, "Buck! Fuck! That's great!" I could feel my release come fast and hard.

"Holy shit…baby…I'm right…fucking there." He breathes heavily.

I feel it when he shoots his load inside me. Damn, that was hot.

He stills, and I collapse down on his chest. We are both

breathing hard and fast, trying to catch our breath.

When I look at him, he's staring at me. "Thank you."

I smile back, "For what? Having sex with you? I think I had a little fun myself."

He laughs, "No, for getting my mind off this place. For making me feel again. I didn't ever think I would feel like this ever again in my life. You changed that. I've been a broken man for so long, I just made it my normal."

He put his hands on my face and pulls me to his mouth, kissing me with a fierce, wanting need. It's as if he's never kissed anyone before and just discovered how wonderful it can be.

Before we can get our wits about us, there is a knock on the door.

Buck yells, "Just a minute."

I pull away from Buck, make my way around the room and collect my clothing, pulling it on as fast as possible. Buck fastens his jeans and looks at me, "What the hell am I supposed to do about a shirt?"

I laugh softly, "No idea."

With his shirt open down the front, he makes his way to the door and opens it to JC.

"What's up?" He looks from JC to me and back to JC.

"The FBI has shown up. They want to talk to you both. They may have something."

"Good, we'll be up there in a few minutes. Thanks, JC."

JC nods and heads back through the barn.

Buck looks at me, "Well, that was close. Shall we?" He motions to the door.

"What about your shirt?"

He shakes his head, "I'll grab one when we get to the house."

Chapter Sixteen

"Sorry about that," I giggle a little.

Buck slaps my ass, "No you aren't." He smiles at me, and we head back to the house.

Chapter Seventeen

Buck

Kristie and I follow JC back to the house. I run upstairs to change my shirt. When I get to my office, it is full of cops.

I look around the room and find JC standing by the back door. He steps forward and introduces me to the agent. "This is Buck Stover. Buck, this is Terry Hannagan with the FBI."

I stick my hand out, "Nice to meet you, Terry. I hope you have some good news for me."

Terry raises his eyebrows and looks at me, "I wouldn't exactly say good news. This is the most bizarre case I've seen in a long time."

"How so?"

"I've never known anyone to kill someone and dump their body on a specific place the way that the bodies have been dumped on yours. This is very personal to whoever's doing it. We've gone over your list of employees since you took over the ranch. Do you happen to have a list of employees prior to you taking over the ranch?"

"Jack and I gathered a list up and gave it to JC," I respond.

I look at JC, "Do you have the list?"

"Yeah, it's on my phone. I'll forward it to you, Terry." JC took out his phone.

Terry nods toward JC, then looks at me. "Can you tell me anything about any of the victims? Do you know them? Are they people that have worked for you? Anything you can tell us that might be helpful."

I look down at the ground and shuffle my feet. "I can't think of anybody that works for me that would do this kind of thing. I can't think of anybody that worked for my father that would do this kind of thing."

"Well, if you think of anything, give me a call. Here's my card." Terry hands me his card.

"JC said you might have a lead?" I ask.

"We have a few things that we're looking into, but right now I wouldn't even call those leads."

"I will continue to think. But right now, I just can't think of anybody that would do something like this."

"Do you have any enemies, anybody that would want to harm you or someone in your family, or make it look like you're involved? Because right now, it looks like you're involved," the agent points out.

"What the fuck. I'm not involved. Somebody's dumping dead bodies on my property and you think I'm involved?"

I feel Kristie's hand on my shoulder, and I turn to her, "What the fuck are they thinking."

"They have to look at all possibilities, Buck. That doesn't mean you've done anything wrong. We know you haven't done anything wrong, and this is not your fault. How about we go into the living room and rack our brains? See if you can't come up with something."

I shake my head and turn to walk out of the room, following Kristie.

JC says, "Buck. Don't take this personally. This is not on you. We all know that you would not be involved in something like this. Get with your guys. See what they know. See if there's anything they might have seen or heard. Has anybody around here pissed anybody off that you know of?"

I shake my head, turn around, and follow Kristie out of the office and into the living room. Jewel and Emma are sitting in the living room talking. They've gotten very close since Emma got here.

"What are you two up to?"

"We're discussing whether Emma would like to go back to Austin with me." Jewel looks from Emma to me to Kristie and back to Emma.

"Why would Emma go back to Austin with you? She goes to school at TCU."

Kristie interrupts, "Maybe Emma needs a change?"

I look at Kristie, Emma, and Jewel again and shake my head. "Whatever."

I walk over to the minibar and pour myself a Scotch neat. I turn back and look at Jewel, "Can you think of anybody who worked for Pa who may have a grudge against our ranch?"

Jewel shakes her head, "Not off the top of my head, but I can think about it for a little bit. I was so young. I don't really know any of the guys that were working for Pa at the time."

"Is there anybody that has a grudge against you?"

She gives me a funny look, "Grudge?"

"Yeah, have you pissed somebody off that we need to know about? Some guy you stood up. Some girl you stood up. Somebody you've pissed off could be doing this shit."

Kristie puts her hand on my forearm. Every time she touches me, it calms me down. "You're asking everybody, right? You're not just asking Jewel."

"What the fuck? Yes, I am asking everybody. Jewel just happens to be sitting here. That's why I'm asking her. What the hell is wrong with everybody?"

Jewel stands from her sitting position on the couch. "If I could think of anybody that might have a grudge against me or anybody else in this family, I will let you know. But right now, I can't think of anybody that I've pissed off enough to want to kill people and dump them on our ranch."

I take a deep breath, "I'm sorry Jewel, this whole thing has got me frustrated. I don't know what to do. If you can think of anybody that might have some kind of a grudge against one of us, please let me know. If you can think of anybody that worked here before Mom and Dad died, let me know that too."

Jewel walks over to me, hugs me, and looks me in the eyes. "I'm sorry that this is happening. They will find out who's doing this, and everything will be back to normal."

I kiss the top of her head and hug her back. "Thank you, squirt."

Jewel laughs, and Emma laughs.

I look over at Emma, "How are you doing, Emma? I haven't talked to you in a couple of hours. Everything going okay?"

Emma smiles for what seems like the first time since we left that horrible place, "I'm doing much better now, Buck, thank you very much. And thank you for letting me stay here. I really appreciate it. It has helped me get to feeling better about myself."

"Do you think it's a good idea for you to go to Austin, to go to school instead of TCU?"

"I don't know, but I do think I need a change. I think it might help. Jewel told me so much about the school in Austin that she's going to. I think it might be a good thing for me."

Kristie pulls Emma into a hug, "Whatever you decide to do, Emma, we will back you 100%. We're here for you, and you can think of this place as your home too."

I look at Kristie, and she looks at me, smiling, "That's okay, right?"

I get a smile on my face for the first time in a while. "Absolutely babe. Whatever you want, you get."

"You may regret saying that mister."

Kristie walks over and hugs me. Emma and Jewel start laughing. I think my spirits have been lifted a little bit. Now I have to think of all the people who've worked for us. All my employee records are in my office, where the police are working right now.

Mitch, Morgan, and Brock walk in about the time I pour myself another glass of Scotch. "You boys wanna drink?"

In unison, they all said, "Hell yeah!"

Jewel, Emma, and Kristie all look at each other and then at me. Kristie said, "We would like a drink as well."

"I'm right on it, babe."

As I'm starting to pour the drinks, Mitch, Morgan, and Brock gather around the bar. Mitch looks at me, "How much longer before the police get out of here?"

"We're fixing to have a family meeting and discuss that very thing."

Brock pipes in, "Oh, goodie."

Nobody laughs.

Family meetings at the Stover Ranch are synonymous with ending in fist fights. We'll see how this one goes.

I hand each of my brothers a drink and take Kristie her drink. Mitch hands Jewel her drink, and Brock hands Emma a soda. Everybody has a seat, and I'm standing by the fireplace. As I look around at my brothers, sister, girlfriend, and houseguest, I feel like a dictator.

"Okay everybody, here's the situation. The FBI are going to be here for a while. JC is keeping us posted on what they're doing. They seem to have a couple of leads. Hopefully, we can get this wrapped up soon. I'm getting really tired of finding dead bodies on our property. As for our ranch, we will continue our day-to-day operations as if nothing has happened."

Brock looks at me. "Buck, how are we supposed to run our ranch with police and FBI running all over the place?"

"Good question, but we're gonna have to try. We've gotta get this solved, so we know who's killing these people. That means the FBI and the police have to be here for a month. We're just gonna have to deal."

Jewel's next to speak up. "Big brother, I need to get back to school. I've got one year left, and I want to end on a good note. I can't stay here for a month, and Emma's wanting to go check out the college too. What are we supposed to do?"

"Jewel, I'll have someone escort you and Emma back to Austin and see if anyone can stay with you. I'll see what we can do about getting a couple of guards, maybe they can stay and rotate every twelve hours."

"Oh goody. I get to be babysat. I'm twenty-two. I don't need babysitters. Nobody's after me."

"Not that you know of. This is just a precaution. We'll send a couple of guys down there to hang out with you until you're break or until this case gets solved."

Jewel leans back against the back of the couch, huffing.

"Emma if you want to go with Jewel to Austin, we will make arrangements for you to be there. If you want to stay here, we're fine with that as well. Just let me know what you wanna do."

Emma shakes her head but doesn't say anything.

"Okay guys, we're going to be on high alert until JC and the FBI figure this case out. Watch everything around you. Watch everybody. If you can think of anybody that worked here prior to mom and dad's accident, please give me their names, so I can pass that on to the FBI. They keep asking me about people who worked here before mom and dad's accident."

Morgan pipes up. "What if it's nobody related to the ranch? What if it's just somebody killing people and randomly, placing them all over our ranch? What if it has nothing to do with our ranch or anybody on it?"

"That's a fair question, but I don't know the answers. I don't know if they've looked at anybody other than people who have been related to the ranch, I'll check it out and see."

Mitch looks at me, "Buck, you know we're going to be here for you and the ranch, and you know we're gonna do everything we can to make sure everyone is kept safe. However, we still have a ranch to run. How are we supposed to go on business as usual when we have dead bodies showing up every other day?"

"We do our best, we do our jobs, and we get it done regardless of what's going on around us. I don't know what else to say."

I look at my brothers, my sister, Kristie, and Emma, and

wonder how we got here, how we ended up in this place at this time—trying to figure out why dead bodies are showing up. I shake my head. Have no clue.

"Dinner's ready," Rooster yells from the kitchen.

"I guess the meeting's over. Let's go eat dinner."

I take Kristie's hand, and we walk into the dining room with Jewel, Emma, Brock, Mitch, and Morgan all following behind us. Not another word is spoken about the bodies being found on our property. Not another word is spoken about the FBI or the police presence. Basically, nobody knows what we're doing. At this point, it's a waiting game.

Chapter Eighteen

Kristie

L ife around here has been interesting. Everyone has been walking around like paranoid robots.

It's been a week since Emma, and I came to stay with Buck.

I leave for work wondering why this family is going through all this. Who could be killing all these people?

I talked my boss into moving me to the Big Springs Hospital. It's been an adjustment, but I like being close to the ranch.

My phone rings, and I answer it from the car. "Dr. Smith."

"Dr. Smith, this is Dr. Norris from Ft. Worth. I was told that you were handling the autopsies from the Stover investigation."

"Yes sir, I am."

"I won't beat around the bush, a John Doe was just brought to me with the same MO as the bodies that have been found in Smithville. Randomly dumped on a ranch just outside of Ft.

Worth," he reports.

"What the heck is going on?" I pull into my parking space at the Big Springs Hospital and sit there thinking about what Dr. Norris has just told me.

"Dr. Smith, I'm not sure. The police were here about a half an hour ago. They told me about the bodies that have been found in Smithville. Can I get your notes on the autopsies you've completed? I'll compare your notes to mine and see what else is similar."

"Of course, I'll fax them right over."

"Thank you."

We disconnect the call, and I call Buck.

"Hey babe, what's up? Are you okay?" he asks.

"Yeah. Um, I just got a call from the M.E. in Ft. Worth."

"What's wrong?"

"He just received a body. Killed and dumped the same way the bodies on the ranch."

"Wow! I'll pass this to JC and let him decide what to do," Buck decides.

"Okay, I just thought you would like to know."

"I do. Thanks for calling. I miss you already."

"I miss you too, baby. I'll be home as soon as I can."

"I love having you here with me. I don't want you to ever leave." Buck's voice drops a little bit.

"I love being there. Why are you talking so low all of a sudden?"

"I'm at the corral and the men are waiting on me to finish some inoculations on the new babies."

"So, you don't want anyone to hear you talking to your girlfriend. I see how it is. You don't want anyone to know how sweet you are."

"I'm a hard ass out here in the field. But with you, I'll be sweet all day long."

"You don't have to be sweet all the time. I kinda like that bad ass man," I giggle.

"Oh baby, I can certainly be a bad ass if you want me to," Buck leads on.

"Can you show me some of that bad ass stuff in the bedroom?"

"You got it, babe. You just wait, I'm going to tear you up tonight."

"I look forward to it. I need to run. I need to fax the reports to the Ft. Worth doctor."

"Yeah, I need to go too. I'll see you later tonight."

I kissed the air loud enough for him to hear me, and he did the same thing.

"Later babe."

"Later." I hung up the phone, gathering my purse and briefcase, and heading to the hospital.

* * *

As I'm heading back to the ranch at the end of my day, I'm almost to the entrance when there is a loud explosion.

I look off to the south, where there is a ton of smoke bellowing toward the sky, and it looks as if it's near the barn.

I punch the gas pedal and haul ass down the long drive. When I reach the house, I see where the smoke is coming from and where the explosion happened.

The secondary barn that is just south of the barn is in flames. I jump out of my car just as the fire engine comes barreling down the drive and heads straight for the fire.

I search around, looking for Buck and the others. Jewel and Emma are standing on the porch. I run up to them. "What the hell happened?"

"No idea. We were all in the living room when it happened. The boys ran out to see what it was. I called 9-1-1," Jewel explains.

"You have no idea what happened?"

"No, the FBI guys all ran out after Buck and the others. I'm just glad that it was a building we don't use." Jewel acts as if this kind of thing happens all the time around here.

Looking from Jewel to Emma and back to Jewel, "So everyone is okay? No one was out there when it happened?"

Jewel looks at me, "No one was out there. Buck was telling us that the FBI had put up surveillance cameras, hopefully, they'll be able to see who did this."

"Lord, I hope so. This is getting out of hand. First the dead bodies, now this. What in the world is going to happen next?" I curiously ask.

Jewel laughs, "Ma always said not to say that because something..."

She was cut off by another explosion just behind the first explosion. The three of us duck, and Emma screams.

I look out to where the firemen are trying to put out the first fire and notice several men running toward us. I couldn't determine who they were, but they were hauling ass to the house.

Two more fire trucks come barreling down the drive and head straight for the fires.

All four of the Stover brothers are running toward the house and the five other men, I assume, are FBI and JC.

Buck, Mitch, and Brock reach the porch first, with Morgan

behind them.

Buck yells, "Get in the house."

I didn't wait for anyone, and I ushered Emma into the house with Jewel on our heels. The men come flying through the door, and we all converge into the living room. The FBI and JC are right behind the other men.

The detective, Terry Hannagan, stood before the fireplace and looks around the room. We all took seats, and the guys are standing around staring at the poor detective.

Terry speaks quietly, "We have some video feed from just before the first explosion. We have some good pictures of four people roaming around in various locations. I'm going to show the pictures to everyone, one on one, and see if anyone recognizes any of the people in the pictures and videos. I just need you all to be patient."

Buck steps forward, "Terry, what about the explosions that went off so close to the house? What did they use?"

"I don't know. We'll have the fire inspector do his report and I'll let you know."

"Damn," Buck whispers under his breath, but I hear him.

I stand, "Thank you agent. We'll wait on you to call us when you feel it's time for us to see the pictures."

Buck looks at me and whispers, "Thank you."

I just give him a weak smile.

Terry and the rest of the FBI men leave the room and head back to Buck's office.

JC comes up to Buck and me, "Guys, this is taking things a step further. These people are getting way too close to the house. I think you all might need to leave the ranch for a while."

"JC, I have a ranch to run. I have cattle to feed, daily. I have men to take care of on this ranch. How the hell am I supposed to do that from somewhere else?" Buck was almost yelling.

"Buck, I understand. But for the safety of everyone here…" He points to Jewel, Emma, and me, "… I think you need to consider everyone."

I can see that Buck is frustrated. I move to him and put my hand on his arm, "Babe, I think JC is right. We are way too close to the explosion. What happens when they get closer to the house?"

Buck's eyes were a darker blue, and he looks mad and sad simultaneously. "I'll get you girls out of here for now. I'll ensure you have security with you at all times. I'm not going to get run off my ranch, but I will take you girls into consideration."

Jewel speaks up, "Buck, I think I need to head back to school. I may be safer there. Emma can come with me. You can send however many security people you want with us, but I'm leaving in the morning."

Buck looks at her, and then back at me.

"Babe, I think she's right. They will probably be safer in Austin." I smile at him and hope that it helps his demeanor.

"Fine. I'll call the security company out of Big Springs that I was going to use. I'll see if they can send at least four men with you girls."

"Thanks Buck. We're going to head up to pack." Jewel hugs Buck, and she and Emma head up to their rooms.

As the girls walk up the stairs, Buck pulls his phone out of his pocket and calls the security company.

I walk up to JC, "What should we do? Can't we just stay here? Buck is not going to want to leave, and neither are any of the other boys."

"I think it's a good idea if you all leave until we find out who is doing this."

"I'll try to convince him to leave, but it won't be easy."

JC shakes his head at me and walks back over to the FBI guy in Buck's office.

I'm standing in the living room, watching the guys move and talk in Buck's office, but I can't get my thoughts together. Living around here is interesting, that's for sure.

* * *

I finally head upstairs and sit on Buck's bed.

When he enters the room, he smiles. "Damn, you look good sitting there."

I smile back at him, "What's going on downstairs?"

Buck sits down next to me on the bed, "Each of us went in and looked at the pictures and videos the FBI collected. None of us could recognize anyone in them. I have no idea who or why anyone would kill people and then set off explosions." Buck put his head in his hands and leans his elbows on his knees.

I place my hand on his shoulder and scoot up next to him, "They'll figure out who it is. I'm sure of it."

He looks over at me, "They are running the pictures through facial recognition at the Bureau but hadn't come up with anything by the time I came up here."

"Buck, JC suggested we leave. What are you going to do?"

"I'm not leaving, and neither are any of the boys. Jewel and Emma will leave for Austin in the morning with security. That leaves you, and I'm not willing to have you stay alone somewhere without me. So, I guess I'm in a bit of a spot."

"I'm staying wherever you are. I'll be fine here with you."

His phone beeps like he has a message. He leans over and kisses me gently on the lips. Then he pulls his phone out of his pocket and checks the text.

"It's from JC. One of the people in the pictures has been identified. He wants me to come downstairs."

"I'm coming too." I jump off the bed.

Buck grabs my arm and pulls me to him as he stands, "I love you. Thank you for being here with me and being so supportive."

"I wouldn't be anywhere else, and I love you too."

He leans into me, putting his left hand on the back of my neck, and his right arm snaking around to my back. He holds me looking deep into my eyes before pulling me closer to him, and his lips touch mine. It's a needy, wanting kiss. He needs me to be here for him and to understand how much he wants me. I feel it in my heart.

I pull back from the kiss and stare into those icy orbs, "Buck, if you ever hurt me, I will hunt you down and castrate you just like you do those bull calves."

He smiles, "Honey, I don't plan on hurting you ever. I plan on being with you for the rest of my life."

My eyes got big, "Kyle Stover, was that a proposal? Because if it was, it stunk."

He laughs as he takes my hand, "No, it was a statement of fact. One day, when all this shit is over around here, I'll make it official. But you should know, you are mine and no one else. I want you. Now, come on, let's go see what they found out."

As we walk down the stairs, the house was eerily quiet. I couldn't even hear Jewel or Emma. I have a strange feeling in the pit of my stomach that something big is about to happen.

Chapter Nineteen

Buck

With Kristie attached to my side, we walk into my office. I see JC and Terry leaning over the computer at my desk.

Terry looks up at me as we walk into the room.

"Buck, think we have a good lead. I need you to look at this person's face and see if you know who they are. I know I've already had you look at the pictures, but this one is a little bit better, and maybe you'll recognize who it is."

I walk around the desk and look over Terry's shoulder. "I have no idea who this person is. I've never seen them before in my life."

"His name is Stan Milford. He's part of an organization out of Amarillo called the Wayward Militia."

"What the hell is a militia wanting with my property? Why are they doing this?"

"Do you know anything about this militia?" Terry looks at

me.

"I've never heard of them, so no."

Kristie steps up, "I've heard of them. They're a mean group. If you don't believe what they believe, they'll kill you."

Terry shakes his head, "Exactly. They're kind of like a cult. They lure homeless people into their group, and they teach them their ways. If they don't like what they're saying or doing, they kill them. We have a file big enough to fill a large filing cabinet. But we never can pinpoint any of them to make an arrest, until now."

"What do you mean until now?" Buck looks confused.

"We now have pictures of some of their guys. I don't know how high up these guys are in their organization. We've been able to identify this man as being a part of the militia, and I'll bet money the other three are with them."

"Okay, so let me get this straight. This militia out of Amarillo kills people when they don't believe in what they believe in, and then they just dump bodies wherever. My property looked like a good place to dump some dead people. What about the explosions?"

"Yeah, I'm not sure about the explosions. That's something new. They haven't done that before. I need to see your brothers."

Kristie looks at me and says she'll find them.

"Thanks babe." Then she leaves the room.

I look at Terry one more time, "Why on Earth would a militia wanna be dumping bodies on my property all the way over here by Big Springs? Amarillo is at least 250 miles from here."

"The only thing I can figure is, they're spreading out into new territory."

"So, this doesn't have anything to do with me, my brothers,

or my ranch."

"I wouldn't say that. That's why I want to talk to your brothers, see if they know any of these people that we're looking at, now that we have a clear picture of who they are."

About the time he said that all three of my brothers walk into the room.

I step back and let Terry do his job.

Terry looks at my brothers and asks, "Okay, I need each one of you to come around here and look at this picture and tell me if you know who this person is or if you've ever seen them anywhere around here."

Mitch took his turn and steps behind Terry to see the picture on the computer. "Nope, never seen him."

Brock took his turn next. "Sorry, I've never seen him before."

Morgan was the last one to take his turn. "Holy fucking shit!"

I look at Morgan, "You know him?"

"Yeah, I know him. He was in my unit. We were in Afghanistan together. He's a piece of shit person. Thought everybody owed him something."

Terry looks at him, "You mean to tell me this man was in your unit. Why would he have a grudge against you?"

"Probably because I told him to go to hell, and he was a piece of shit. He never pulled his weight when he was supposed to, and he was never where he was supposed to be. He always thought he knew more than anybody else, including the captain. But everybody in my unit gave him hell."

That's the most words Morgan has said since returning from Afghanistan.

Terry looks at me, "There's our connection. Somehow, he found out this was Morgan's place. He's trying to get back at

Morgan for something."

Morgan is now pacing back and forth, mumbling under his breath. I can't make out anything that he's saying.

Terry looks at Morgan. "Can you tell me anything about this man that might help us figure out what he's doing?"

Morgan stops pacing. "Shit, I don't know. I can't think of anything. Like I said, the man was a piece of shit. I tried to stay away from him all the time. He was always in somebody's business, always wanting to know things. Hell, I couldn't even tell you where he lived."

"Okay, if you can think of anything, come tell me. Let me know as soon as you think of anything."

Terry's computer dinged. While he was pushing buttons on his computer, we're all standing around trying to figure out why these men wanted to do this to Morgan.

"Morgan, come look at these other three men. We just got hits on them. Do you know any of these?"

Morgan walks around behind Terry and looks at the computer screen again.

Terry flips through the pictures one by one. In the last picture that he flips to, Morgan shouts, "Fuck! Son of a bitch!"

Terry moves his chair back and stands. "What is it? What are you seeing?"

"That man right there. That man was my Sergeant. He got all buddy buddy with several of us guys. We didn't think anything about it. He was the Sergeant."

"That's Toby Sinclair. He's known as one of the main guys in the militia. Did he tell you anything about himself?"

"Not really. We always were just shooting the shit, you know, hanging out. Tried to make the best of where we were and what we were having to do. I don't know that he ever really said where he lived or where he was from."

"Morgan, if you can think of anything else, anything at all, come see me. I'm gonna get my superiors on this ASAP."

Morgan just shakes his head.

Terry looks at me, "I gotta make some phone calls. Do you mind excusing me for a few minutes?"

"No problem." I start heading out of the office, and my brothers follow me into the living room where Kristie is waiting for me.

Kristie stands as we walk into the room. "I can tell by the looks on your faces that something is up. Is everything okay?"

"Yeah babe, everything's fine. We were able to recognize two of the men, or Morgan was able to recognize two of the men."

"That's a good thing, right?"

"I think so. Terry's calling his superiors now. Hopefully this will be over pretty soon."

Kristie walks over to Morgan, "Are you okay? Do you need to talk to someone?"

He just shakes his head, walks to the bar, and makes himself a drink.

Kristie looks at me, "I'm gonna go upstairs. If you need anything, let me know."

I go over to her and kiss her on the forehead. "Thanks babe."

Then she disappears up the stairs.

I say to Morgan, "Hey, fix me one of those too."

Brock and Mitch both say the same thing.

"Look Morgan, this is not your fault. This is not on you. You can't help what those assholes are doing."

"Those assholes were part of my unit. They're doing this because they hate me. So yeah, this is on me."

Mitch says, "Morgan, listen man, there is no way this is on

you."

"You have no idea what we went through over there. You have no idea what I'm thinking. But those stupid assholes that are leaving dead bodies and setting off explosions, that's on me. I treated those assholes like they were nothing because to me, they were nothing. I didn't give a shit. So yeah, it's on me." Morgan storms out of the house.

Brock looks at me. "Should I go after him?"

"No, let him be. He needs to cool off." I walk to the door and watch Morgan storm to the bunkhouse.

"This is some messed up shit," Mitch says.

"You got that right bro," Brock agrees.

"Once the FBI figures out where they're at. This will all be over with. We just gotta hang in there for a little bit longer." I down the rest of my drink and put the glass on the table next to the door. "I'm heading to bed."

The FBI finally left the property, and I need some alone time with my girl.

When I open the door to my bedroom, she is lying on the bed with her back facing me. She looks so cute, curled up in my gigantic king-sized bed. I never want her to leave.

I strip down to my boxers and crawl under the covers next to her.

I snuggle into her warm body. She turns to face me. I put my hand on her cheek, "Sorry, I didn't mean to wake you up."

"I wasn't quite asleep yet. I was waiting on you." Her hand snakes around my neck, and her lips start kissing my chest and working her way up to my lips. Just the touch of her hand makes my dick hard. Her lips are on mine, and her hand slowly grazes my chest. She works her way down and grabs hold of my cock. She begins to massage my dick with her warm hand.

I slowly pull back from the kiss, gazing into her eyes.

"God, you're amazing." I wrap my arm around her waist and pull her over on top of me. She giggles. Her long chestnut hair makes a curtain around us. It's just her and me, nobody else.

"I need you more now than I ever needed anyone."

Both my hands find her ass, and I grab two handfuls.

"I need you too, Buck." She lowers her mouth to mine.

She's perfect. Her mouth opens, and my tongue darts in, slowly caressing her tongue and exploring every centimeter of her mouth. My hands are massaging her butt.

She begins to move her hips as I'm massaging. She pulls back from the kiss and sits up, straddling me. I can feel her wetness on my dick. She places her hands on my chest and begins to move her hips back and forth across my cock.

"Woman, you are playing with fire."

She smiles, "Am I?" Her hips start moving faster and faster.

My dick swells more, and I didn't even know it could get that hard. I stop her movements with my hands on her hips, "Sit on my dick, baby. I need to feel you. I need inside you right now, or I'm going to lose it."

She lifts slightly, taking my cock in her hand and positioning it at her entrance. "You want this?" She begins to move the head of my dick across her wet hot pussy. She still has my cock gripped in her hand, torturing me with it.

"Fuck yeah." I'm getting frustrated. I need her now.

"Say the magic word." She gives me a seductive grin.

"Oh fuck."

Her hand continues to stroke my cock and tease me with her wetness. "That's not the magic word."

I give her an edgy look. "Fuck me!"

"No." She continues her torture.

176

My cock is weeping for her pussy. I can feel the pre-cum as she slides my dick across her pussy.

That's it. I take her by the waist, and in just a second, I flip her over, and now I'm on top.

She gasps, "Shit, that was cool." She giggles again.

"Now I'm in control." I give her a sadistic look. "Spread your legs for me baby. Let me in."

She moves her legs apart, allowing me to slide between them.

My dick is so hard, it is starting to hurt. I want this woman so bad. "See what happens when you play with fire, darlin'? You lose."

"Oh, I don't think I lost anything." She wiggles under me, pressing up against my cock.

"You little wench, you planned it this way. Just for that, I'm not giving you my dick."

Her bottom lips pouts out, "Pretty please."

"I like it when you beg. But you are going to have to wait now."

I lower myself down to her lips, nipping at her mouth with my teeth. Then I move to her neck, just between her shoulder and ear, kissing my way down. Taking both her breasts in my hands, I pinch her nipples as I continue to kiss my way down her body.

She begins to moan and buck her hips up.

"You like that don't you. You are so receptive to my touch. Tell daddy what you want."

"I want… you to fuck me. Please," she's begging.

"Oh, I will, just not yet. I have to punish you first for that little torture session."

I move my mouth down, taking in one of her hard nipples, and I bite down just enough to make her scream a little.

Her body moves up, as she arches her back into my touch.

I continue biting and moving down her body, kissing and sucking every inch of her. My mouth finds that hard little nub, and I suck it hard and fast into my mouth.

She screeches, trying not to make too much noise.

I smile into her wetness, "Let it go babe, scream."

I continue my torture on her clit, sucking and licking, flicking it with my tongue. Moving down to her folds, I lick, tasting her warm juices. She's dripping wet.

Her hips come up to meet my mouth as I continue licking from her pussy to her clit. Sucking her hard clit into my mouth, she screams my name, letting go of her orgasm.

I look up, her head is thrown back, her back arched, and she's breathing heavily. Her hands have fisted the blankets next to her.

I keep sucking. "Come for me again baby, you taste so good."

"Buck, please, I need you... inside me now, please."

As I continue licking, I insert two fingers into her pussy, moving in and out, and hitting her 'G' spot. She's so close to coming again.

"Let go baby." I keep moving my tongue against her clit and sucking it into my mouth, as my fingers play and probe her insides.

Her body is moving with every move of my fingers. She throws her head back again and explodes her essence on my fingers.

Gently removing my fingers from her pussy, I sit up and suck my fingers clean of her juices while she watches me.

Her breathing is heavy, and she looks so good lying under me.

Moving up her body, kissing as I go, I center myself over her with my dick waiting at her entrance. I move the head around, and it hits her clit.

She takes in a deep sharp breath.

"You want this?" I ask, moving my cock back and forth, teasing her.

She shakes her head.

"I need your words Kristie, tell me what you want."

"I need you inside me now, right now."

"I'm guessing you liked the punishment?"

"Oh yes, you can punish me like that any time."

I smile at her, "Spread those beautiful legs baby, I'm coming in."

I don't give her any more warning, I slam my dick deep inside her.

She yelps.

My hips begin to move, and her hands find my ass and squeeze.

Her hot juicy wetness envelopes my cock like a warm blanket on a cold night.

"I'm home. You are my home." I move faster, burying my cock deeper and deeper inside her.

"I'm... coming... Damn... this is... good!" Kristie is moving with me.

"Come with me babe... you ready? Damn!"

I feel my balls tighten, her pussy clinches my cock, and that's all it takes. I shoot cum deep inside her and hold still, buried deep in her hot goodness. I wrap my arms around her and pull her to me. Kissing her neck, head, and lips, I don't move other than that.

Pulling back slightly, I look into her eyes, "I love you with all my heart."

She smiles at me. "I love you too, Buck, with all my heart."

I hold her tight. We stay like that for several minutes, enjoying the sweet aftermath of our love for each other.

I finally say, "I need to go get cleaned up."

"Yeah, I need to pee too." She smirks.

Moving slowly, my dick slips from her warmness, and I groan. I put my forehead to hers. "You are one amazing lady. Thank you for loving me."

She smiles. "Thank you for loving me. I think you are amazing as well."

I give her a quick kiss on the lips and move off of her. I get up and head to the bathroom to clean myself up. She follows, so she can do her business.

We meet back at the bed, and I put a soft, thick blanket over the wet spot so neither of us has to lie in it.

We both get back into the bed. I pull the covers over both of us, and in minutes, I drift off to sleep knowing that this woman is mine. I am the luckiest man on earth.

Chapter Twenty

Kristie

I'm startled awake by someone beating on the bedroom door. I feel the bed move, and Buck gets up. I watch him put on his boxers and fling the door open. "What the fuck do you want?"

Mitch is standing at the door.

I glance at the clock. It says 3:30.

Mitch is breathing heavily. "Morgan's gone. I can't find him anywhere. After last night, I thought he would be okay, but he's disappeared. I don't know where he went."

"What do you mean he's gone? I thought he went to the bunkhouse."

"We did too. When we got to the bunkhouse, he wasn't there. I thought maybe he went out for a drink or to clear his head or something, but he hasn't returned yet. Now I'm getting worried."

"Give me just a minute." Buck shuts the door and turns to

me. "Sorry we woke you. I've gotta go see where Morgan went."

"Of course, yes, I'll come help you find him."

"No baby, you go back to sleep. I'll get the guys from the bunkhouse to help me and Mitch look for him." He walks over to me and puts his hand on my cheek. Buck leans down and gives me a sweet, tender kiss.

"Buck, the more that are looking for Morgan, the faster we can find him."

"Baby, I do not want you out there looking for Morgan because I don't know where those fucking militia people are. I don't want anything to happen to you. Please stay here, and I'll stay in touch with you by cell."

"Yeah, I guess that makes sense."

"Thanks baby. I'll keep you informed of where we're at and what we're doing at all times."

"Just keep me posted, baby."

I watch as Buck rushes around the room, gathering his clothes and getting ready to go out and find his brother. What a nightmare! I get up and put on some clothes. I walk down the hall to make sure Jewel and Emma are okay.

Buck comes out of the bedroom, "I'll call you as soon as I know something." He kisses me on the forehead. "I love you."

"I love you too. Be safe."

Buck hauls ass down the stairs, and I hear the front door close. I open the door to Emma's room. She's sleeping. I close the door softly, walk down to Jewel's room, and knock gently. No answer. I gently open the door. She's sleeping as well. *Well, at least Mitch didn't wake them up.*

Now that I'm awake, I guess I can get myself some coffee. I'm not going to be able to sleep now, since I'm going to be worried about where Morgan is.

I walk into the kitchen, flip on the light, make my way to the coffee pot, and start making some coffee. The house is quiet. Eerily quiet. I can hear the trees rustling in the wind just outside the window.

While I wait for the coffee to brew, I walk to the double doors at the back of the house. I look out across the field behind the house. I think I see something, but I'm not sure. I go flip the light off and walk back to the doors. I watch the trees to see if I can see what I thought I saw. Something moving? Maybe it's just my imagination with everything that's been going on around here.

Oh, there it is again. I see it. There's something out there.

"Hey, what are you doing?" a voice comes from behind me.

I jump, startled, and throw my hand to my chest as I turn and see Rooster standing at the kitchen door. "Shit, you scared me."

"I'm sorry Miss Kristie, I didn't know you were down here. What are you doing down here anyway?"

"Mitch woke us up this morning, they can't find Morgan. Or Morgan hasn't made it back from wherever it is he went. I don't know. So, I decided to come down and make me some coffee while I wait for Buck to call me."

"I'm sorry, I didn't mean to scare you. Let me get the coffee…" his voice trails off.

"Yeah, I've already started it. It's not a big deal. What are you doing down here so early?"

"I'm usually in the kitchen by 3:30 or 4:00 in the morning to get started on breakfast and then preparing lunch and you know, getting ready for the day."

"Wow, I didn't realize you got started so early."

"I have to get started early around here. The crew is usually up around 4:30 or 5 o'clock. I have to have breakfast ready."

"You are one busy man." I smile at Rooster.

Rooster looks at the coffee pot. "Looks like the coffee is ready. You want me to fix you a cup?"

"Oh, for heaven's sakes, I can fix a cup of coffee for myself." I walk to the coffee pot, grab a cup from the cabinet above, and start adding the cream and sugar.

My cell goes off. I look at it, and it's Buck. I press the answer button. "Hey, did you find him?"

"Not yet. We've looked around the bunkhouse, in the barn, and he's nowhere to be found around here. We're gonna drive into town and see if maybe he was at the bar or something?"

"Please be careful. Do you think you need to call JC and see if he knows anything?"

"Not yet. I'll call him if I can't find him here in a couple of hours," Buck says.

"Let me know if there's anything I can do. I'm awake, so I'll do whatever I can."

"Thanks honey. I'll be in touch. Love you."

"I love you too." I click the off button on my phone.

I hear Rooster behind me, shuffling his feet, and I turn.

"They haven't found him yet?"

"No, not yet. They're going into town to see if maybe he had hit a bar or something. I don't know."

"I'm sure he'll be fine. Morgan knows how to take care of himself."

Rooster starts his morning routine by turning on the oven. I watch for a few minutes as he moves around the kitchen with ease.

"I'm gonna take my coffee and go sit on the front porch. I'll probably be awake to watch the sunrise."

"If you need anything let me know."

"Thank you, Rooster." I take my coffee and head to the front porch.

As I'm sitting on the front porch, I'm listening to all the sounds around the ranch. It's quiet, but there's still some noise. I hear the cows moo in the distance. I hear the wind blowing through the trees. As I look across, I see lights from the bunkhouse come on. I had no idea that ranch life started so early.

As I'm sitting here listening to all the different noises around the ranch, I hear something a little disturbing like leaves rustling and a branch crack. I turned my head to the right, where the noise was, to see if I can see anything. It's still fairly dark. I don't see anything. But I know there's something out there. The hair on the back of my neck stands up. I can feel it.

I stand to go back in the house when I hear it again. More rustling leaves, more something. There's something out there, I can sense it.

I walk to the edge of the porch and look over. It's hard to see around the house. It's so dark. No, I can't see anything.

It's probably my imagination. I turn to go back into the house when a large person confronts me. I gasp and jump back.

Before I can do anything, this person is on me. His hand is over my mouth, and I can't move. My eyes are wide, and I'm trying to see who it is. He's got black clothes, a black mask, and all I see are his eyes—dark, mean brown eyes. All I can think is not again.

He picks me up off the porch, my feet dangling, and starts hauling me down the steps. His hand is still on my mouth. I can't scream, but I'm trying to kick. I'm trying to pull at him. I can hardly move. Whatever I'm doing is not helping. He's huge. He takes me around the side of the house and takes off through the woods, carrying me. His hand slips a little bit, and I bite down as hard as possible. He screams. Not very loud, but he screams. Maybe somebody heard it.

"You bitch!" Then he slaps me across the face.

I try screaming, but as soon as I open my mouth to scream, his hand is back over it.

"You be a good girl, and you might make it out of this alive."

Great. Just great. I'm getting kidnapped, again. What the hell? I continue fighting this man, kicking, and clawing.

He stops. He has me tight against his body.

I can't move.

He wraps one of his legs around my legs, so I can't kick him. He's fiddling with something behind him. I don't know what he's doing. All of a sudden, there's a rag over my face.

"Told you to be a good girl bitch, and you might come out of this alive. Now, I don't know. Goodnight, sweet princess."

After I hear his words, everything went black.

Chapter Twenty-One

Buck

Mitch, Brock, and I head into town to see if we can find Morgan. He does this from time to time. He just disappears. But right now, is not a good time to disappear.

"Did either of you see him last night when you went back to the bunkhouse?"

"No, he wasn't in there," Brock says.

"Nope. I checked everywhere in the bunkhouse, and he wasn't anywhere to be found," Mitch agrees with Brock.

"What the fuck does he think he's doing? We do not have time for this. We got people dropping dead bodies right and left, exploding our buildings, and he wants to disappear."

"Since he found out two of his unit people were involved in all this, he kind of went weird. I don't know, not sure why. All I know is, I think he took it personally," Mitch says.

"Yeah, I noticed he was acting strange after he saw the

pictures of the two guys that were in the militia that were the same men in his unit. Damn it."

I pull up in front of the bar. It's four in the morning. I don't see any of our vehicles. There's nobody around. "Keep an eye out for his truck, guys."

I slowly move down Main Street. I'm looking down the alleys and in the streets. I don't know where else he could be. The cafe doesn't open for another hour. So, I know he's not there.

Mitch speaks up, "There's his truck. Take a right up here."

I make a right at the next corner, and we circle around where his truck was seen.

"Yeah, that's his truck," Brock says.

I pull up next to it and park. We all three steps out of the vehicle. We walk around his truck. It's locked. He's not in it, "What the fuck?"

I pull my cell phone out, I hate to call JC at 4:00 a.m., but I have no choice. I hit JC's number.

He answers, "What the fuck do you want? Do you know what time it is?"

"Yes, I know what time it is. I'm out here on the street looking at my brother's truck, and I can't find my brother."

"Which brother?"

"Morgan. After he found out about the two men involved in the militia that were in his unit, he disappeared. Thought maybe he came into town and got drunk last night. We found his truck four blocks from the bar, but no Morgan."

There's a beep on my phone. I look, it's Rooster. "I got another call from the ranch. We're on Fourth and Main."

"Give me fifteen, and I'll be there."

I click over, "Rooster, what's up?"

188

"Buck, umm… Miss Kristie's missing?"

"What do you mean missing? She was there when I left thirty minutes ago."

"She was in the kitchen when I came in to start breakfast. She had made some coffee. We had some conversation, then she took her coffee out to the porch. I went to see if she wanted some more coffee, and she wasn't there. Her coffee cup is still sitting on the table next to where she was sitting, but she's gone. I looked all over the house. I looked outside. I looked upstairs. She's not here."

"What the fuck? Is Jewel and Emma still there?"

"Yes, I just checked on them. They're both awake now because I woke them up to see if they knew where Kristie was. I've called down to the barn, none of the guys down there have seen her."

I rub my hand down my face. What the hell is going on? First Morgan, now Kristie. "Thanks Rooster, I'll be in touch."

I hit JC's number again.

"I said I'd be there in fifteen."

"Now Kristie's missing. She's not at the ranch. They've looked everywhere for her, and she's not there."

"I'll call Terry and see what's going on, see if they can get the video from the ranch. Hang tight, I'm on my way."

Mitch looks at me, "What the hell?"

"I'm guessing the militia is a little pissed off, and so they're retaliating. JC is calling Terry. He will be here in a few minutes."

Ten minutes later, JC pulls in next to my truck. He gets out and shakes my hand. "Terry's pulling all of the video from the cameras on your property. Maybe we can at least see what happened with Kristie. I've got a team headed over this way to fingerprint Morgan's truck, and I've got the city police department pulling all video from this street and the surrounding streets. We'll find them."

"I can't lose either one of them JC. They have to be found… in one piece and alive."

"Man, we are trying. Like I said, we're going to go over the video surveillance from the ranch and from town."

"I know. Morgan is fragile. He really needs counselling after what he went through in Afghanistan. Kristie is the love of my life. I've got to get her back."

Mitch comes up behind me and puts his hand on my shoulder. "Let's head back to the ranch until we hear from Terry or JC. Let them do their job, they'll find them."

I stand there, staring off into space in disbelief. I can't believe Kristie's been taken again, and now Morgan's missing. God, they better find them.

Mitch, Brock, and I climb into my truck, leaving JC to take care of Morgan's truck. We head back to the ranch in complete silence.

I pull the truck up to the house and look at Brock and Mitch. "Go to the bunkhouse and tell the boys what's going on. Let them know we are working business as usual, and I will take care of finding Kristie and Morgan."

Mitch looks at me. "Man, we can help."

I throw my hands up. "I don't wanna hear it. I know you can help, but apparently, there's not anything we can do. I'm gonna check on Jewel and Emma. Please, just go fill the men in on what's going on."

Brock and Mitch get out of the truck and head to the bunkhouse.

I sit there looking at the porch and the house, glancing

around at the property. Everywhere I look, I see Kristie.

The sun is starting to come up. Wishing that I was sitting on the front porch with Kristie watching it. Where the hell are you, Kristie? Come on. "You've got to tell me where you are." I mumbled, hoping the universe would send her a message.

I step out of the truck and slowly make my way up the stairs and into the house. I hear talking from the kitchen, so I head in there. Jewel and Emma are sitting at the bar drinking coffee and listening to Rooster while he fixes breakfast. "Good morning, everyone."

Rooster pauses. "Hey boss, any word?"

I shake my head no.

Jewel moves from her spot at the bar, comes over to me, and hugs me. "They'll find her, don't worry. We've got cameras all over this place now. They'll find her."

I look at her. "Morgan's also missing."

Jewel steps back from me, "What do you mean missing?"

"We found his truck in town. JC is having it fingerprinted and pulling video from the cameras in town."

Jewel steps back a little bit more. "Okay, they'll find them both. Don't worry, surely all of the people that work for the FBI, and the city police department can find two human beings."

"I hope so little one, I really do. I don't want to lose either one of them. I'm gonna go take a shower. If anyone calls, come get me please."

"Okay, I'll let you know," Jewel's voice cracked a little. I know she's upset about Morgan.

I look over at Emma before I head upstairs. "Are you okay?"

"Yes, they'll find them. Just like they found Kristie and I before."

I give them both a nod and head upstairs to take a quick shower. I turn the water on, strip down, and look at my reflection in the mirror. For the first time since Mom and Dad died, I feel helpless. "I can't lose another woman. I can't lose Kristie, and I sure as hell can't lose my brother."

I step into the shower and let the water pour over my head. I stand there for what seems like an hour, trying to decide what I should do. "I've gotta do something. I can't just stand here all day in the shower. But what can I do?"

Finally, I wash off quickly, rinse, turn the water off, and step out to dry off. Going into the bedroom, I change into some clean clothes. "There's gotta be something we can do." My phone rings.

"Stover."

"Buck, it's JC. Hey, we have a lead. You want in on it. Terry said you could go."

"Hell, yeah."

"Meet me at the precinct. We're leaving in twenty minutes."

"I'm on my way." I finish getting ready, run downstairs, and into the kitchen. "They have a lead. I'm headed to the precinct to go with them. Nobody leaves this property. Don't even leave the house."

I didn't wait for anybody to answer. I just haul ass out the door and into my truck. I'm heading down the driveway, and call Mitch. "Hey, they have a lead. I'm headed to the precinct."

"What do you want me to do?"

"Protect Jewel, Emma, and Brock."

"On it, brother. Keep me posted."

I disconnected the line.

Fifteen minutes later, I'm pulling up to the precinct, and JC is walking out the door. I jump out of my truck and into his.

Chapter Twenty-One

I look at JC as he starts the truck. "So, what's the lead?"

"You'll see when we get there."

Not another word is spoken for the next hour and a half."

Chapter Twenty-Two

Kristie

My head is pounding. I'm trying to sit up, but I can't. Why can't I sit up? I try opening my eyes. It feels like they're glued shut. I give it a few minutes and lay there.

Trying to open my eyes again through the slits in my eyes, I see light. I'm in a room. It's not a room. It looks more like a cellar. It smells musty and dirty. I have no clue where I'm at. What happened? Where am I now?

I finally get my eyes open enough to see. They're trying to adjust to the dim lighting in the room. As I look around, it's most definitely some type of cellar or basement. I hear somebody moan. Still from my lying position, I look to my right. Oh my God, it's Morgan.

My mouth feels like cotton. I can't even say anything. I try swallowing. I try to get some saliva in my mouth, so I can at least say something. I finally try to sit up again. I finally manage to get myself in a sitting position and look over again. It looks like he's been beaten to hell. His face is all bruised. His eyes are black and blue, and he has a bloody lip.

I lick my lips, trying to get some moisture in my mouth. I squeak out, "Morgan."

He doesn't respond.

I don't want to be loud because I don't want anybody to hear me. But I try again, "Morgan. Morgan, wake up."

He moves slightly, but he's still not waking up.

I scoot off the disgusting mattress and gingerly make my way over to Morgan's cot. I put my hand on his arm.

"Morgan, wake up. Morgan, it's me, Kristie, wake up." I whisper.

Morgan turns his head back and forth like he's in a nightmare. He looks terrible. Who the hell did this to him?

I look around the room. It's small and dingy. There are some makeshift shelves on the opposite side of the room. We're not tied up, thank God. I gently stand and make my way over to the door. I put my hand on the handle and try to turn it slowly, but it doesn't budge.

"Shit. It's locked. Of course, it's locked. Somebody's fucking taken us. Why does this keep happening to me," I talk to myself.

I put my ear to the door. I'm trying to hear anything, any movement, any sound. There's nothing.

This room has no windows, just a door and some rickety shelves.

I make my way back over to Morgan's cot. I sit on the edge next to him. I take his hand in mine and pat it.

"Morgan, I need you to wake up. Come on Morgan, you can wake up." I continue to pat his hand.

He moves his head back and forth and moans. I'm sure he's

in pain.

"What the hell am I going to do? Who is doing this shit to me? Us? This is ridiculous."

I look back over toward the door. There's some light coming from underneath it. Does that mean there's a light in the hall? Or is it daylight? Hell, I don't even know.

I look back at Morgan. His eyes are starting to open. I don't see how he's going to open his eyes very much at all, they're so black and blue and swollen.

"Morgan, wake up. It's me, Kristie. Morgan, what happened? Why are you all beat up?"

"What?" his voice comes out raspy.

"Morgan, you've been beat up. We're in some kind of basement or cellar or something. I don't know where we are. Can you please wake up?"

His eyes barely open. He barely gets the words out. "Kristie… what happened?"

"Morgan, you've been beat up. Do you know who did this to you?"

"I can't remember."

"Do you remember getting here?" I ask.

"No. I don't remember anything. How did you get here?"

"Buck, Mitch, and Brock all went out looking for you. I was sitting on the front porch drinking coffee, and I heard a noise. When I went to see what it was, there was a man, and he grabbed me. He must have put some kind of something over my nose because the next thing I know, I'm waking up here. Wherever here is."

"The last thing I remember was pulling up to the bar in town. I don't remember anything after that."

"I don't know who these people are or what they want."

I stand and walk around the room. I turn, and Morgan's trying to sit up. I rush over to him and help him sit on the cot's edge. "Don't move too fast."

"Trust me, I won't. My head is pounding."

"It looks like you've been beat up pretty bad. Your eyes are both black and blue and pretty swollen. And you have a cut lip."

"What the fuck?"

"I'm not exactly sure what happened. All I know is we're stuck here, and I don't know where we are."

We're each standing by Morgan's cot and hear a noise coming from the other side of the door.

Morgan looks at me and whispers, "Lay on the cot and act like you're still asleep."

I do as he says, and he also lays down on his cot. We both close our eyes as the door opens.

"They're still knocked out. How much chloroform did you give them?" a rough voice comes from the door.

A deeper, gravelly voice answers, "Enough to knock him out, so we didn't have to put up with his bullshit. That motherfucker gave me a black eye."

"Well, the bitch bit my hand. I have permanent teeth marks. Do you think we should wake him up?"

"I'd like to wake that bitch up and fuck her, but Ned said we had to wait."

I'm facing the wall from where I'm lying on the cot, and my eyes pop open. A tear forms, and now, I'm more scared than before.

"Looks to me like she has a nice ass. I wouldn't mind fucking that."

They both laugh.

The gravelly voice guy spouts, "Soon, we'll have a good time with her. And I can't wait to make that asshole pay for how he treated me in Afghanistan. Motherfucker was cruel. I'll show him just what cruel is."

"Come on, let's go. We can check back in about an hour. They should be awake by then."

I hear the door close and what sounds like a key or something locking us back in.

I don't move from where I am for several minutes. Then I hear Morgan move on his cot.

I watch Morgan stand from the cot and walk to the door. He's studying it through his very swollen eyes. "I think I can get this door open."

"And what happens when we get out of here? We don't even know where we are. Did you hear what those men said?"

"No, we don't know where we are, but we can at least get this door open and see where it goes. And yes, that's why we need to get out of here."

"Good point, what do you need me to do?"

"The hinges are on this side of the door. If we can get the bolts out of the hinges, we can get the door off. Let's just hope they're not rusted on."

Morgan looks around the room like he's looking for something that he can use to open the door. He walks over to the shelf and starts running his hand across the top, down the sides and on the inside.

"What are you looking for?"

"Something that I can use to pry those hinges off." He continues inspecting the shelf.

I stand and watch because I don't know what else to do.

Morgan looks over at my cot, "Help me move this cot over

by the shelf, so I can look on the top and see if there's anything up there."

Morgan and I pick the cot up. It's not heavy. We move it over to the shelf. He carefully steps on the cot to look up on the shelves, so he can see in the back.

"Bingo!" he says excitedly but in a whisper. It's the first smile ever I've seen on his face.

Morgan pulls what looks to be a file of some kind, only large. "What is that?"

"It's a metal file that you use in a metal shop. It's similar to what we use when we shoe horses. But it's got a sharp end on it. It's just big enough and long enough that it just might work."

Morgan goes to the door and places the sharp end of the file at the bottom of the top hinge. He hits the bottom of the file upward with the heel of his hand, and the bolt starts to move upward.

"Ohhh my gosh, it's working," I whisper excitedly.

He then places the pointy end under the top of the bolt and starts hitting it up again with the heel of his hand.

"Morgan, don't hurt your hand."

"I don't give a fuck about my hand. I wanna get out of this place."

For the next several minutes, I watch in amazement as Morgan removes the bolts from the three hinges on the door. He lays the bolts on the floor, takes the metal file, and pries the backside of the door away from the door frame. When he has a good grip on it, he takes one hand on the handle, one hand on the opposite side of the door, and gently pulls.

It makes a squeaking noise, and we both freeze.

I look at Morgan, and he puts his finger over his split lip in order to say shhh. I nod my head at him.

Morgan pulls the door away from the frame enough to see what's on the other side.

"What's out there?" I ask.

"It looks like we're in a basement of a house. There's a small hall and then stairs leading up.

I shake my head, showing that I understand.

"I'm going to try and sneak up the stairs and see if I can hear anything or see anything."

"Morgan, please be careful."

He shakes his head and moves the door enough to squeeze through the small opening, which is difficult because he's a large man.

I'm so scared right now. I start pacing around the small room, waiting for Morgan to return.

It's taking him forever. It feels like I've paced back and forth around this room for an hour when I hear the door squeak slightly again.

I look up and Morgan is pulling himself back through the door. Then, he leans it back against the door frame.

"So, what did you see?"

"I didn't see much of anything, but I could hear voices on the other side of the door upstairs."

"Did you hear anything that could help us?"

"I heard them making plans to dump another body. But it wasn't on our property, it was somewhere in Ft. Worth. They were discussing what they were going to do with us, but I couldn't make out much. All I know is, we need to find a way out of here and soon."

Tears form in the corner of my eyes, and I can't help it. After what I heard that man say about me, I can't go through something like that.

Morgan looks at me, takes my arm, and pulls me into him, "It's going to be okay. We are going to get out of here, and I will not let them hurt you. I'll fight to my death before I allow them to lay a finger on you."

"That's what they want. They will kill you and do… do despicable things to me." The tears start to flow.

"We don't have time for tears right now. We only have a short time before they come back and check on us. When I was out there, I noticed a small window. It's too far up for both of us to get out, but I can lift you."

"No, I'm not leaving without you."

"Kristie, listen to me. You will, and you will go get help."

I'm shaking my head no and backing away from him.

"Look, it's the only option I can see that we have. I have no idea where we are, but you have to get out and find help."

I wipe my eyes, straighten my shoulders, and say, "Fine. I'll do whatever you say. I just don't like it."

"Point taken. Now, let's see if we can get out of here."

I watch him move back to the door. He puts his ear to it to see if he can hear anyone. "It's quiet, so let's do this."

I shake my head and follow him through the opening of the door. We are standing in the small space at the base of the stairs.

I look up to see where the window is. It's about three feet above the door that we just came through.

I whisper, "There is no way I can reach that window."

"I'm going to put you on my shoulders. Then you are going to stand up on them and reach the window. I'm six-four and you are five-six or seven, right?"

I shake my head. "Five-six."

"That's eleven feet ten inches. That will get you there. You just have to be able to get that window open."

"Oh shit! I'm afraid of heights. I can't do this."

Morgan puts both his hands on my shoulders and bends down, so he was eye level with mine. "You can and will do this. We have to get help."

I know my eyes must be huge, but I just shake my head in agreement.

"Good. Now, I'm going to bend down, and you are going to get on my shoulders. Then you will use the wall to help you stand. Once you are up there, be very careful but get that window open," he's whispering while he gives me the instructions.

"What if I can't get the window open?"

"We'll deal with that if it happens. Just do your best."

I shake my head.

"Ready?"

Again, I shake my head, slightly this time.

Morgan bends down, and I crawl up his back to sit on his shoulders. He starts to stand, and I grab his head.

"Give me your hands."

Carefully, I give him one hand at a time, and now I'm grasping both his hands and trying not to pass out.

"Okay, I'm moving to the wall."

He moves as close to the wall as he can.

"Put your hands on the wall," he's still whispering.

One hand at a time, I place them both on the wall.

"Now, I'm going to lift you up by your feet."

"What?" I say a little louder than I mean to.

"Shh."

"Sorry."

"I'm going to take each of your feet, on the bottom, and put them in the palms of my hands. I will then lift you up, so that you can stand on my shoulders."

I think this guy is nuts, and he isn't going to be able to hold me up like that. I don't care how many muscles the guy has.

"I'm afraid you'll drop me."

"I can bench press over three hundred pounds. Unless you gain an additional hundred and fifty pounds or so, I think I'm good."

"Oh."

He moves his hands to my feet, lifting one foot and placing it on his shoulder, then doing the same with the other. I'm now kind of squatting on his head.

"Now, walk your hands up the wall and stand up."

I take a deep breath and start inching my way up the wall.

Just as I'm in a standing position, we hear the door upstairs start to open. I freeze.

A man standing at the top of the stairs is looking back into the room, "I'm just checking." It's the gravelly voiced guy that said he wanted to fuck me.

"It hasn't been long enough. Come on, we need to finish this hand of cards."

"Fuck, fine… but I'm going down there after this round."

We hear the door shut again.

I feel Morgan's shoulders slump a bit like he's holding his breath. I know I was, and I let out a soft sigh.

"Hurry," Morgan says.

I can now see out the window and try to open it. "It's stuck."

"Keep trying."

I push on the window frame all around the edges. The paint is chipped, and it's not hard to remove the paint from it. After

I get that done, I try to push it up again. It starts to move.

I keep trying until the window opens enough for me to crawl out. "I got it."

"Good. Get out the window and go for help."

"I'll do my best."

"I'm going to push your feet up over my head to help you get up and out."

I feel his hands under my feet again. Then, I'm lifted and pull myself out through the window's opening. I land on the roof.

I stick my head back through the window. "I'm out."

"Be careful."

I nod and slowly close the window back down. When I turn to look at where I am, I'm on the roof of an old house. Shit, how am I going to get off this roof? I hate heights. The roof is not steep, but it has a decent pitch. I start to scoot down until I can see the ground below. All I have on are my house shoes and my pajamas. What the hell am I going to do?

Chapter Twenty-Three

Buck

JC pulls up to the Amarillo Police Department. We get out of the truck and head inside. We walk up to the counter, and the officer behind the desk asks, "Can I help you?"

JC says, "We're here to see Terry Hannagan." He pulls out his badge and shows it to the officer.

"One moment." The officer picks up the phone sitting on the desk.

I look around the precinct, and everyone seems to be moving in slow motion. I'm about to lose it.

The officer hangs up the phone and says, "He'll be right out. Just have a seat." He points to some chairs over by the wall.

I look at JC as we move toward the chairs. "I can't sit. I need to find my brother and Kristie."

"Buck, that's why we're here. Terry assures me that they know where they are. He'll have a plan, and we will follow that plan."

"This is bullshit. They could be dead or… or worse."

JC looks at me, "What's worse than death?"

"Torture."

JC shakes his head. "Come on, sit down, and Terry will be out in a minute."

"It's been hours since they went missing. What if something…"

"JC… Buck…" Terry walks out from some double doors at the end of the hallway and sticks out his hand to JC first to shake, then to me.

I look at him, "How much longer do we have to wait?"

"Come on back. I'll let you in on what we are doing."

Terry moves like a damn snail. It doesn't seem like anyone is in a hurry to find my brother or my girl. My head is spinning with all that could be going wrong.

We follow Terry down a long hall, through another set of double doors and to a large conference room. There are fifteen or twenty people roaming around the room. Terry points to a few seats by a small window and then stands in front of the huge conference room table.

He clears his throat, "Okay everybody, can I have your attention?"

Everyone in the room stops and turns to look at Terry.

"We have four compounds that the militia occupies. Two of those, we've confirmed, are empty. However, two are occupied. Those are the two we're going to focus on. We have two teams. Each team has twenty to twenty-five people. We're going to breach both properties at the same time. We know there are about ten people in one location and about five people in the other location. I'm gonna bet money that Mr. Stover and Dr. Smith are being held in the location where there are more people."

I can't believe how long this is taking. They need to get my brother and my girl. I stand and start pacing.

Terry looks back at me. "Man, we're going to get them back. It just takes time to organize everything so that we can do this the right way."

All I can do is shake my head and stare at him.

Terry turns back to his group. "We roll out in twenty minutes. Everybody be ready."

The entire room started moving and head to the doors. I watch all the commotion.

Terry comes up to us. "Let's go. I want you both in protective gear."

JC and I follow Terry out of the room and down a long corridor. He walks into another room full of weapons, vests, and other police stuff I didn't want to know about.

JC looks at me. "We'll get them back. Here, put this on." He shoves a vest at me. I put it over my head, then Terry comes up behind me.

"Here." He starts tightening the Velcro straps from the back to the front.

"You guys wear these all the time? Damn, these are uncomfortable."

JC and Terry smirk at me. "Ya get used to it."

Men and women were getting weapons and checking ammunition around the room. It was total chaos.

"Let's move. Green team with me, blue team with Mac." He looks at me. "You stay close to JC. Do not go rogue on me, or I will shoot you."

I know he is kidding, or at least I hope he is. I know better than to leave JC's side.

JC and I follow Terry and the other FBI agents down a long hall and out a back door into what looks like a parking lot for nothing but police cars. There are plain, black SUV's. There were a ton of cop cars. Terry's team had six of the black SUV's. I didn't bother looking around to see what Mac's team had. I assume the same thing.

JC and I jump in the back seat of the black SUV that was for Terry. Terry was in the passenger seat, and another guy was in the driver's seat.

Terry turns slightly to look at us as the vehicle moves. "This is Dyson. He's my partner."

Dyson nods in the rearview mirror and flew out of the parking lot, taking a right onto the street behind the police department.

I look behind us, and there is a line of black SUV's right behind us with their lights on. No sirens. I look forward as I watch Dyson swing around a corner, he's now heading South toward I-40.

Terry turns slightly in his seat again. "The compound that we're headed to is about fifteen miles west of Amarillo, out in the middle of nowhere."

I ask, "And where is Max's team headed?"

"The other compound that we found with the five people in it, is southwest of I-40 about five miles. It's not very far. They'll get to their location before we do."

"Then how are you going to storm both compounds at the same time?" I'm confused.

"We have locations set up just outside of the compounds where they can't see us, and they don't know we're there. Once everybody's in position, we'll give the go, and we all move in at the same time."

All I can do is shake my head. I'm so nervous that my leg is shaking.

JC's looking at me like I'm crazy. "It's gonna be okay, we're gonna get them back."

"I just hope they're there."

"Me too brother, me too"

I look out the window as we get on I-40 and head west. All I can think about, is my girl and my brother, and bringing them back home safely.

* * *

We finally make it to a patch of trees. Everyone exits their SUV's, and Terry gathers everyone around.

"Okay troops, this is what we've trained for. We've got two hostages, a dark-headed female, Dr. Kristie Smith, and a former military man, Morgan Stover. You studied their pictures. We do this right. We get them out safely and alive. So, don't do it wrong."

I look at Terry. "Some pep talk dude."

Terry just smiles. When his smile fades, he looks at me. "I need you to stay here. Preferably inside the SUV. You are not to come anywhere near where we are. I'm serious. If I see you out there, I will shoot you. You stay here, and we will bring them to you. You're a civilian. I cannot have your blood on my hands."

I look at him with a funny look on my face. "Unless you're the one shooting me, right?"

Terry smiles again. "Yeah."

I just shake my head and stand next to the SUV.

Terry presses his ear and says something I can't make out

from where I'm standing. Then all the officers gather around Terry.

"I need you, you and you." He points to three officers. "Go around the north side, spread out, and cover that end." Then, he looks at some other people, "You three go to the east, cover that side. You seven move to the west. Spread out. The rest of us will stay on the south side. I want this place surrounded. Stay in the tree line and don't be seen. Move quietly and efficiently. Do not go until I give the order. Mac's team is in place and waiting on us. Go!"

Once he said the word go, everybody moved quietly. I couldn't believe everybody is finally spreading out and doing what I wanted them to do hours ago.

I stand back by the SUV and just watch. They disappear into the tree line within minutes, and I can't see one person. JC moved out with Terry. I'm standing here alone, just waiting. I step to the back of the car and start pacing. I don't know what else to do. All I know is, I need my family back.

Chapter Twenty-Four

Kristie

As I'm standing on the roof, I hear voices down below. I freeze. I can't make out exactly what they're saying. I try to gently move close to the edge without making any noise or falling off, I can't get caught.

It's very quiet out, and they're kind of mumbling. I can smell cigarette smoke. They're standing right below where I'm at. I can't move anywhere.

I'm literally sitting just above a door because I hear it open. Another person joins the two that are smoking. Him, I can hear. It's the really gruff-sounding guy that came into the basement earlier.

"That bitch we're holding, damn, she's fine."

"Yeah, I can't wait to get a hold of her."

"What are they going to do with that asshole that's down there?"

"Oh, the boss has plans for him. Apparently, they were in the military together, and he was a fucking asshole to the boss."

"Damn, hope I'm around to watch that."

From a distance, I hear another voice.

"Hey assholes, get in here."

I hear shuffling feet, and then hear the door close again. I'm frozen to my spot on the roof. I just sit there, listening. I want to make sure there is nobody else down there. I sit there for what seemed like hours, but I know it's only been a few minutes.

I start gently scooting over to the edge of the roof. I lay on my stomach and peer over the edge. It actually doesn't seem like it is that far to the ground. I decide I will have to hang off the roof's edge, drop onto the ground, and hope I don't break anything.

It is clear nobody is down below, so I gently move my legs around, staying on my stomach until they're at the roof's edge. I take a deep breath and dangle my feet off the roof. I gently edge myself over the side and am hanging by my fingers. I take a deep breath and let go. My feet hit the ground, and I think I hurt my ankle.

I mutter, "Shit!"

I stay squatted down, listening for any movement from inside the house. When I hear nothing, I stand and hobble over to the side of the house, pressing myself against it. My ankle hurts, but I don't have time to cry right now.

There's a tree line across from the house, about fifty yards. Surely, I can make it that far. I start hobbling as fast as I can toward the trees. The next thing I know, there's a man running toward me. Who the hell is that? He has a gun, and he has a vest on. Oh, thank God, it says FBI. I run to him as quickly as possible with my twisted ankle.

He looks at me. "Dr. Smith?"

"Yes, I'm Kristie Smith. Thank God! Somebody's gotta go get Morgan."

He throws the gun he is holding on his arm around his back by the strap. He picks me up like a sack of potatoes and hauls ass back toward the tree line.

"You've gotta go get Morgan."

He sits me down, and I wince. "Ma'am, I've gotta get you to safety. We've got the place surrounded. We are about to go get Mr. Stover."

"Oh, thank God."

The man touches his ear. "I've got Dr. Smith. I'm taking her back to the vehicles."

Then he looks at me. "Ma'am, can you walk back to the vehicles, or do I need to carry you?"

"I'll try and walk, thank you."

He holds his arm out for me to take a hold.

I try to put as much weight on his arm as I can to walk. "How far is it back to the vehicle?"

"About half a mile."

"Oh, shit."

The cute FBI agent looks at me and smiles. "Do you want me to carry you now?"

I'm still dressed in pajama shorts, a tank top, and no bra. I'm mortified. I bite my bottom lip and look up at him. "My ankle really hurts."

"Come on, let me carry you." He takes me in his arms with little to no effort, and carries me bridal style, and heads off through the trees.

It doesn't seem like it took that long before I see several black SUV's just beyond the tree line. Once we make it through the trees, I see him. My Buck comes running towards us.

"Thank God! You're safe." He removes me from the FBI agent's arms and nods to him.

I wrap my arms around his neck, bury my face in it, and feel him move. For the first time since all this started, I start crying. I'm not a crier at all, but this has been way more than I have ever been through, and I couldn't help it. Tears flow.

"Shh…babe, it's okay. You are safe now. I've got you." I hear him open a door and slide me in.

I don't want to let him go.

He slides in next to me and pulls me back onto his lap, cradling me in his arms. "Baby, cry it out. You are safe now. I've got you."

I lift my head from his neck to look into his eyes. "I was afraid you wouldn't find us in time."

"The FBI was on it as soon as you went missing. We called them when I found Morgan's truck in town and no Morgan. Is he okay?"

"He was when I left. I heard those assholes talking about how 'the boss' was going to make him pay for what he did to them in the service."

"How did you get out?"

I look at him, "Morgan. He was able to get the basement door off where they had us held. We found a window, and he boosted me up so that I could slide out of it. Please tell me they are going to get him out of there."

"They are. There are twenty FBI agents, and JC, surrounding that place right now. They have a plan, and I know he'll walk out of there."

I lean back into him. "Thank you for coming to get me."

"I will always come and get you. I love you." He kisses the

top of my head.

We sit like that for quite a while. I must have drifted off to sleep because the next thing I know, Buck is moving me off his lap.

"What's wrong?"

He points out the front window of the SUV. "Look."

I look up through the window.

Several men are running toward us, and Morgan is with them.

"Oh shit! He's bleeding." I move to get out of the truck and forget about my ankle. "Shit!"

Buck is right behind me. "Stay here. Don't move."

Buck takes off after his brother once he notices I'm standing near the truck and not moving. I watch as Buck grabs Morgan's arm and wraps his arm around Morgan's waist to help him.

What the hell happened after I left?

The agents, JC, Buck, and Morgan, make it back to the SUV.

"What happened?" I look at Morgan.

He smiles at me, blood dripping down his face, and his hands are bloody. "After you left, those assholes came down and found you were gone. They weren't happy." His words were a little muffled through the blood dripping out the side of his mouth.

Buck looks at Terry, "Do you have a first aid kit?"

"Yeah, it's in the back. Come on." Terry takes off to the back of the vehicle.

I hobble slowly to the back. "Oh Morgan, I'm so sorry."

"No, I'm glad you got out. They were coming to do... things to you. That's what made them mad. You were gone."

Buck's face looks at me. "What?"

"They had threatened to... well let's just say... it wasn't

215

pleasant," I tell him.

I think Buck's face turns nine shades of red.

"I'm fine. They didn't touch me," I assure him.

Buck looks at Terry. "What about those assholes? Did you get them?"

"Yes, there were nine men. All dead or arrested."

"What about Sinclair and Milford? Were they in there?"

He looks down at the ground, "No, but we'll find them."

"You better find them before I do," Buck's voice is harsh and flat.

I put my hand on his shoulder. "We're okay. We got out."

"Yeah, but those fucking assholes are still out there."

Terry says, "We'll find them."

They continue to clean Morgan's cuts and bruises. I move back to the door of the SUV and sit up in the seat.

I want to go home, take a hot shower, and lie next to my man.

Chapter Twenty-Five

Buck

I find a blanket in the SUV to wrap Kristie in. She was in her pajamas. Her pert nipples were hard, and I know I shouldn't be turned on right now due to our situation, but damn, the woman is gorgeous.

After wrapping her in the blanket, I text Mitch, letting him know we found them alive and mostly well. And to let him know we were heading home.

Morgan, Kristie, and I sit in the back seat of the SUV as we leave the area, finally being done with this whole situation. Terry's not with us, but JC is. JC turns and looks at me.

"They were only able to collect the members of the militia that were in the cabin. The two that were in Morgan's unit were not there. They also weren't in Mac's raid. They have an all-points bulletin out for both of those two men. I just wanted you guys to know."

"So, we're still not out of danger yet?"

"It's just a matter of time. They'll catch'em," JC said, and then turns back, looking out the windshield.

The ride back to Amarillo was very quiet. Once we got back, we move from the FBI vehicle into JC's. As we pull out of the police precinct, JC says, "They'll find them Buck. They always get their guy."

"I'm sure they do, but in the meantime, what do we do if somebody tries to kidnap my girl or beat up my brother again? Or we find more dead bodies on our property? Or another building blows up? Are they gonna find them before somebody else gets hurt?"

JC is silent for a few minutes before saying, "I get you're frustrated. I totally understand. You may need to up your security around the ranch. Think you can do that for a little bit until they find those two guys?"

"Yeah, I can handle it. I hate to, but I can handle it. We should feel safe in our own home. But none of us feel safe right now."

JC shakes his head. "I understand, Buck. Sorry you're having to go through this, but we've got to be able to keep you safe while we're trying to find those two idiots."

"Those sons of bitches better be found quick," I'm fuming.

Kristie put her hand on my leg, and I look over at her. Her beautiful caramel eyes glistening up at me. That look gave me what I needed to calm down a little. I take her hand in mine and just squeeze it and smile at her.

The rest of the drive from Amarillo to Smithville is silent.

I watch my brother, Morgan, for a few minutes, and he seems to be withdrawing more into himself, even more so than when he returned from Afghanistan.

Morgan's the middle child. He's the one that is the most irritating. Growing up, he wanted to be the center of attention.

The older kids were doing stuff he wanted to do but couldn't. The younger kids were doing things he didn't want to do. He was just that typical middle child and had that typical middle child syndrome.

I'm just glad to have my brother and my girl back. Mostly in one piece.

We pull into the Smithville Police Department, and JC turns to look at me. "Buck, they will find those guys, I promise."

I open the door to the truck and get out. I help Kristie down, and Morgan gets out on the other side. We head to my truck.

Nobody talks on the drive to the ranch. It's the longest twenty-minute drive I've ever had.

As we pull up to the front of the house, Jewel, Emma, Mitch, and Brock are all standing on the front porch waiting on us.

I step out of the truck and walk around to help Kristie down. I hear the girls suck in a deep breath when they saw Morgan.

Jewel and Emma immediately went to Morgan's side and helped him up the steps. He's limping and looks like he's been in the worst fight of his life.

Brock follows them into the house, and Mitch says to Kristie, "I'm glad you're okay, Kristie. I can't imagine what you've been through in the last twenty-four hours."

She gives him a weak smile. "Thank you."

"Let's get you in the house." I put my hand on her back and escort her through the front door, with Mitch following close behind.

She looks at me. "I wanna go take a long hot shower."

I give her a slight nod. "Okay, baby. I'll be up in just a little bit to check on you."

As much as I want to follow her upstairs, I need to check on Morgan. I watch Kristie walk up the stairs slowly and disappear into our room.

Mitch and I walk into the living room, where Jewel and Emma are fussing over Morgan.

Morgan looks at us. "Man, I'm sorry for all this trouble. If I hadn't treated those two like the assholes they were, we probably wouldn't be going through this shit right now."

"This is not on you, brother. This is on them. They're the ones doing this, not you."

I've never seen Morgan so broken.

Morgan stands from where he's sitting next to Jewel and Emma on the sofa. "I'm gonna go take a shower and lay down for a little bit."

"And Morgan, I want you to stay in the house. In fact, I want all of us to stay in the house until this is over."

Morgan just nods and heads upstairs to his old room, I assume. He never gives in that quickly.

Jewel walks up to me. "He looks bad Buck. I'm worried about him."

"He's gonna be okay, Squirt. We just gotta give him some time to heal."

Jewel looks between Mitch and me. "I've postponed us going back to Austin until I know everything's going to be okay. We were going to go, but after seeing Morgan the way he is, there's no way I'm leaving right now."

"I think that's a wise decision."

I hadn't noticed earlier, but Brock is paying a lot of attention to Emma. I need to keep an eye on those two.

Jewel heads to the kitchen, Emma sits back on the sofa, and Brock sits next to her. Yeah, I'm going to have to keep an eye on them.

I motion with my head for Mitch to follow me. I don't say

anything, but he knew.

We walk into my office, and I close the door behind us.

"We got a lot of things we need to keep an eye on around here."

Mitch smiles. "Yeah, did you see what Brock was doing with Emma?"

"I didn't see him doing anything. I just saw him being very close to her and watching her carefully."

"I'll keep an eye on Brock. It's kind of strange for Jewel to change her plans for anybody. I think seeing Morgan really shook her up."

"I wanna see if we can't get Morgan back out working. Have him run with Jack. Make sure there's at least three or four men riding together when they're checking pastures. And I don't want anyone going anywhere alone. There should be at least two people, even walking across from the barn to the house and from the barn to the bunkhouse. Everyone should have someone walking with them. I don't care who they are."

"I'll get with Jack and the others in the morning and make sure they know."

"I want the family staying in the house until I hear back from the FBI. You boys can sleep here in your old bedrooms instead of in the bunkhouse. Which means somebody's gonna have to keep an eye on Brock. I don't know what is going through that boy's head."

Mitch laughs, "I don't think it's his *head* that we need to worry about." He points to his temple.

"I think he's got to be the horniest of all of us. I've never seen anybody chase more pussy in my life." I'm laugh. "But I don't want Emma to be one of his notches on his bedpost. She's too sweet of a girl to be caught up in his bullshit."

He nods, and then changes the subject, "When all this bullshit is over, I wanna talk to you about possibly building a house for me. We all know which acreages are ours. I think it's time for me to step up and start being more responsible."

I sit there and stare at my brother for a minute and wonder why he suddenly wants to step out on his own. "You got some plans I don't know about, brother?"

"No, I just think it's time for me to get out from under my big brother's apron strings." He smiles at me. "Seriously, I think it's time for me to get out and make sure I've got my own way. I'll still be here. I'll still take care of things around here like I always have."

"All right, I get ya. I understand. You're twenty-eight years old. You wanna be out on your own. But like you said, let's get all this bullshit out of the way first. I don't want you out on that ten-thousand acres all by yourself."

"Thanks man. I'm gonna go check on Morgan."

"I'm gonna go check on Brock, and then I'm gonna go check on my girl. Thanks for your help."

"Anytime, that's what I'm here for."

Mitch opens the door, and we both walk out. He walks upstairs, and I walk to the living room.

Brock is sitting on the sofa, but Emma has left.

"Brock, I need to talk to you for a minute."

Brock looks at me, "What'd I do now?"

"I'm not sure. I need you to maybe stay clear of Emma. You seem to be a little too close, sometimes."

"Oh Buck, I'm not doing anything to her. I think she's nice."

"Yeah, she's a nice girl, and I don't want you ruining her."

"Buck, I promise I would not do that to her. She's too good of a person." Brock looks down at his feet.

Chapter Twenty-Five

"Brock, what's going on? You need to talk about something?"

"Nah, you wouldn't understand."

"Try me, I might surprise you."

"It's nothing. Never mind. I'm going to go up to bed." Brock stands from the sofa and heads to the stairs.

"Brock, I'm your big brother. I'm here if you need me. I need you to know that."

Brock turns and looks at me, nods his head, and then heads upstairs.

What a day this has been.

I'm standing in the middle of my living room with my hands on my hips, looking up at the ceiling, "This has got to end soon."

I take a deep breath and let it out. Then I head upstairs to check on my girl. I just need to hold her.

Chapter Twenty-Six

Kristie

I step into Buck's bedroom, and all of a sudden feel overwhelmed. Everything that's happened to me in the last twenty-four hours has thrown me for a loop. What am I even doing here? Why am I even bothering with him? Because he's wonderful to me, that's why I've fallen in love with him, heart, and soul.

I'm not sure how long I just stand there. It seems like a minute, but I know it had to have been quite a while. I finally throw the blanket on the bed I had been wrapped in for the last several hours. I walk into the bathroom, turn on the shower to let it warm, and strip off the nasty pajamas I've been wearing since yesterday. They are filthy, and I will burn them.

The steam from the shower starts to bellow out of the top, and I step in under the spray. I am letting the water just run over me and not moving much at all. After several minutes, the tears begin to flow. I can't help it. I'm literally sobbing. I think of what could have happened. What that man said about me, what he wanted to do to me, and I can't stop the tears.

I don't know how long I've been standing here with the water just dripping down my body. It must have been longer than I thought. The shower door opens, and Buck steps in. I lose it again. Tears just start streaming.

Buck's massive arms wrap around me and hold me close to his body. He's whispering to me, "Shhh…let it all out, baby. It's okay."

The tears don't stop. They freaking just continue. I wrap my arms around his middle and hold him. It feels so good to be back in his arms.

I look up into his eyes, "Why do you keep coming after me?"

"I told you, I will always come after you. I love you. You're right here." He puts his hand over his heart.

Then he brings his hands to my face and puts his lips on mine with a soft, gentle kiss. When he pulls back, he says, "You're mine and I will always take care of you. I'm sorry, I've done a shitty job of it up to this point. But from here on out, I will protect you with all I have."

"Thank you. And I love you too, with all my heart."

"You'll have me for as long as you want me. I'm yours."

The water begins to run cooler, and he helps me wash my hair and body. He shut the shower off and reach for the towel hanging on the hook by the shower door.

Buck wraps it around me and helps me out of the shower. Then he dries off as I brush my hair.

I look in the mirror, and my eyes are all puffy and red. My face is splotchy, and I look terrible. How on Earth could he love someone that looks this bad? I turn to face him, damn he's fine.

He walks to me, places his hands on each side of my face, and pulls me in for a sweet, barely there kiss. As he pulls back slightly, he says, "You are the most gorgeous woman on Earth. I'm so glad that you chose me."

More tears threaten to fall, but I hold them back, "Buck, I look…"

"Absolutely amazing." He didn't let me finish what I was going to say.

I start to shake my head, and he stops me.

"Let's go to bed. I want to hold you all night long." He takes my hand, and we move to the bedroom. He pulls the covers back from the bed, turns back to me, removes the towel wrapped around me, and moves me to the edge of the bed.

I start to protest, "Buck…"

"Shhh… we don't have to do anything. I just want to hold you in my arms. I was so scared that I'd never see you again. I need to hold you."

I bite my lower lip and watch the love in his eyes, they sparkle. I shake my head.

He helps me in the bed, covers me, then makes his way around to the other side, pulls the covers back, and slips in beside me. He pulls me to him and holds me.

My hand rests on his chest, and I can feel his heartbeat. It's somewhat fast but not rapid. His lips touch my forehead, gently placing a kiss there, then moving down, kissing my temple, each one of my eyes, and the tip of my nose.

"Kristie, you are the most perfect woman. I know you have had a rough couple of days, and I'm so sorry you got mixed up in this mess. But I'm so glad that you are here with me, right now." He kisses each cheek and then moves to my lips.

He whispers, "I love you, now and forever." His lips tenderly touch mine.

That's it, and I can't stand it any longer. I need this man more than I need air to breathe. I take the kiss deeper. I wrap my hand around his neck, pull him closer to me, and devour his mouth.

"Buck, I need you. I need to feel your body on mine. I need to feel… safe."

Buck moves his hand down my chest, massaging and pinching each nipple.

The sensation goes straight to my pussy.

My other hand finds his hard cock, and I begin to stroke up and down his shaft. This night is going to be about sex, not love. I need it hard, and I need it now.

"Buck, don't be gentle. I need you, now."

He stops his movements, "What? Really?"

"Yes, I need to forget, and I need you to remind me that you and I are one. No foreplay, just fuck me."

He looks into my eyes, then kisses me hard. His mouth lands on mine with force. His tongue is fierce and invades my space with a hunger I've never known.

His body moves so that he is now on top of me. "You sure about this?"

I shake my head. Spreading my legs wide, I move under him, grasp his dick again, and center it with my pussy.

With one hard thrust, he pushes his way into me, hard and fast. He pumps inside me over and over. With each thrust, he pushes harder and deeper within my wetness. One of his hands moves to pinch my nipple hard. His rough hands become a vice that surrounds my breast and squeezes hard.

My hips move up to meet each of his thrusts. I wrap my legs around his waist, locking my ankles, bringing him in deeper each time he thrusts inside me. My moans become screams of his name over and over.

I feel my walls tighten around his hard shaft.

His eyes are on me the whole time, "Come now baby, fucking come all over my dick."

That's all it takes, his words. I come crashing through the biggest and longest orgasm I've ever had in my life.

He stills for a moment letting me come down from the high before he starts pounding and thrusting hard and fast again. "I'm coming, God, yes, your pussy is so good."

I reach around and start clawing at his back, knowing I'm going to come again.

He throws his head back and growls out my name as his own release comes shooting forth.

"I'm coming again, don't stop."

He doesn't. He keeps pushing inside me, not letting up.

My nails dig into his flesh as I come for the second time. I hold onto him, and he holds onto me as we both slow our movements and relax in each other's arms. Each of us allowing the other to slow our breathing and follow our high down.

His head is resting on my shoulder as our breathing returns to normal. He finally lifts his head, "Damn babe, that was intense. That was the most intense orgasm I've ever had. Fuck, that was good."

I smile at him, "It was pretty amazing for me too." My smile fades a little, "Thank you, I so needed that. I just needed some raw animalistic sex, and you delivered."

He lets out a loud laugh, "You are welcome. Any time you need something like that, just let me know. I can be gentle, or I can be as rough as you need me to be."

"Duly noted, sir. Now I need to pee." My emotions are still

all over the place, but I feel better than earlier.

Buck smiles, kisses the end of my nose, and pulls out of me. He moves to the side to allow me to get up, and then follows me to the bathroom. He gets a towel and cleans himself up while I do my business.

We both wash our hands, and he takes a small soft blanket from the cabinet to lay on the bed where the wet spot is. He is so considerate.

We both crawl back into bed. He wraps me up in his arms, and I snuggle down as close to him as I can.

He leans over and kisses my forehead. "I love you, sweetheart."

I kiss the arm wrapped around my chest. "I love you too."

I drift off to sleep a short time later, knowing that this is where I'm supposed to be. Right here, in this man's arms.

Chapter Twenty-Seven

Buck

It has been a month since Kristie and Morgan were taken. We haven't heard anything from the FBI or the police about the two assholes from Morgan's unit. It's like the two disappeared into thin air. I, for one, am not happy about the situation.

Kristie rolls over in the bed next to me. She is stretching, and her pert nipples are poking through her soft t-shirt.

I can't help myself, even though she's asleep, I need my mouth on those beautiful buds. Moving my hand to the hem of her shirt, I gently move my hand under her shirt and roll one of her nipples between my thumb and finger.

She moans.

I lift her shirt and wrap my lips around the nipple closest to me while I continue pinching the other nipple.

Her hips move up, and she continues to moan a beautiful soft moan.

While I suck and feast on her breast, I move my hand down her stomach and slip it into her shorts. She doesn't wear panties to bed, just shorts. My fingers begin to rub and play with her clit.

Her hips start to rise to meet my moves. The faster my fingers move, the faster her hips move. "Oh Buck… please…" she whispers, her eyes still closed.

I start to kiss her neck and suck the sensitive spot between her shoulder and ear. I bite down, then kiss and lick the spot. All the while, my fingers slowly move from her clit to her soft wet folds.

As I slip a finger into her moist wet pussy, she moves her hips up to meet my thrusts. "Buck, please…"

I kiss my way down her body, sucking each of her pert nipples into my mouth before going lower. I kiss my way down her stomach as I continue to finger her hot pussy.

My lips find their way to her hard nub, and I suck it into my mouth. My tongue flicks her clit over and over with a rapid motion while I slip a second finger inside her.

I make a come-hither movement with my fingers hitting her 'G' spot over and over, sucking her clit, hard and fast.

"Buck, I'm… fucking… coming," her voice is strained and getting loud.

"Come for me baby, let go." My fingers are moving faster and hitting her special spot continuously with a bit of force.

"Yes… God… Buck," she screams out.

She comes all over my fingers.

I pull them out as she opens her eyes and meets mine. "Oh… my… God, babe."

I put my fingers in my mouth and suck them clean. "You taste so good. I think I need more."

231

I move my mouth from her clit down to her soaked pussy, and lick. "You got another one for me?"

"Oh Buck, you have no idea how good your tongue is. Yeah… just like that."

My tongue is buried in her wetness, then I lick up, pressing her 'G' spot again. I put my thumb on her clit and rub gently. My tongue moves in and out, and I suck hard.

Pressing my thumb against her clit, I rub harder, and she comes undone. I drink all her juices right down. I start kissing and licking her clit on my way up. I kiss and suck in her nipples as I make my way to her mouth. She loves the taste of her essence on my tongue and sucks on it as I move it around in her mouth.

Her legs spread wide, and I center myself between her gorgeous thighs. I place my hard cock at her entrance. "I love you, Kristie Smith."

"I love you too, Buck Stover."

I slip my dick inside her now soaked, hot wetness, which feels so good.

"Your so wet for me. I can't stop making love to you."

Her hips rise to meet each of my thrusts. I move my hips as I plunge deep inside her wet pussy.

"This…" I wiggle my hips, and my dick expands. "…This is my home. You are my home. Don't ever leave me."

Her eyes meet mine, "I'm home, you are my home too. I love you and won't leave you. I'm all yours." Her hips lift to meet each one of my thrusts.

"Don't stop." Her legs wrap around me.

I get deeper and deeper, moving in and out. I feel her walls tighten around my cock, and my balls tighten. "Come with me."

Pumping in and out faster, we both come together. She coats my dick with her creamy cum, and I shoot mine inside her.

I collapse on top of her but hold myself up by my forearms, so I don't smother her. I kiss her soft and gently, savoring every centimeter of her mouth.

She has her arms wrapped around my neck and holds me closer to her.

Our lips finally part, and I hold her close to me while she runs her hands up and down my back.

I want to stay like this for the rest of my life.

Kristie

This is the most wonderful man on earth. I can't believe he wants me, simple, loner... me. I feel his dick slowly slip out of my pussy and miss that connection. I think I could stay in this bed for the rest of my life.

"Buck, you are so amazing, and I love you so much. I wish we could stay like this and not have to leave this room."

"I don't think either of us could live on sex alone. We do need food." He smiles at me.

"Well, yeah, we do need food. But I want to stay here with you like this and never have to leave."

"I'm pretty sure people would come looking for us if we never left this room."

I swat his back where my hands have been while we made love. "You know what I mean."

He laughs again. "Oh, I think I could make love to you over and over and over. We'll have to try that sometime."

"As much as I want to stay like this, I need to pee." I smile.

"Ummm... you said you wanted to stay this way forever."

I wiggle under him. "Come on, I need to pee really bad."

He moves his hips next to mine, and my bladder is about to burst. "Really?"

I put my hands on his chest and try to push him off me. "Please."

He laughs again but moves off me and rolls over to his side of the bed.

I jump up and run to the bathroom like my 'pants' are on fire. I hear him laughing the entire time.

Buck walks into the bathroom, grabs a towel, then wipes his dick off.

I finish doing my business and wash my hands.

Buck turns the shower on. "Come on, take a shower with me."

"Umm… that sounds nice."

He grabs my hand and pulls me into the shower, shutting the door behind us. He pushes me up against the back of the shower and presses his body into mine.

I can feel his erection grow next to my stomach, and I push back at him.

Buck puts his hands under my arms and pushes me up, and I wrap my legs around his waist. He pushes my arms up and holds them with one hand while he moves his fingers to my clit.

"Mmmm… God my clit is so sensitive. Work me baby."

He moves the hand holding my hands down to my ass, "Don't move your arms. Keep them up there."

I smile, "Sure." I know what is coming.

His hands move to my waist, and he lifts me gently so that his dick is centered at my pussy, then he sits me down on his hard cock.

Chapter Twenty-Seven

"Oh… my… yes!"

His mouth finds one of my nipples and sucks it into his mouth, he moans as he sucks.

My head goes back as he sucks harder on my nipple and moves his dick in and out of me. "God… please let me touch you."

"No." He left one nipple and moved to the other. His hands are on my waist, lifting me up and down on his dick.

My legs squeeze tight around his waist, and I feel my pussy walls tighten around his hard shaft.

"I'm coming!" I scream his name.

"Hold on to my shoulders, I'm coming with you."

He slams into me over and over as we both come together.

I wrap my arms around his neck as we both allow the water to roll over us. We hold on to each other as the water cascades down our bodies, and we don't move for several minutes.

He finally lifts his head from my shoulder. "I'm letting you down now."

Gently, he eases me up, and his dick slides out of my wetness. He takes the shampoo, squeezes some in his hand, and starts washing my hair. After he rinses it out, I put some in my hand and wash his. We continue this routine through washing each other off, rinsing, and then he turns the water off.

He reaches out of the shower door, pulls the large soft towel in, and wraps it around me. I step out as he grabs the other towel and wraps it around his middle, knotting it at his waist. I can see that perfect 'V' that leads down to what I now know to be the perfect dick.

This man is the best, and I can't wait to spend the rest of my life with him. He's my world.

Three months later...

Buck

The work on the ranch started being more normal. Everyone is still walking or riding in doubles wherever we go. No one goes anywhere alone.

Morgan has decided to get counseling and has been seeing someone in town for the past month. It seems to be helping, but he has a long way to go.

Jewel and Emma went back to Austin. Emma enrolled in school for the new semester, and Jewel has been showing her around campus. Jewel starts her last semester, while Emma will be in her sophomore year. They have security with them at all times.

Brock has been moping around like a lost puppy since the girls left. He might have a thing for Emma, but Kristie will make sure he doesn't get too close.

Mitch seems to be going through something now, but he won't talk about it. He's been moody and sometimes downright mean to everyone around. That's not like Mitch, but he took what happened to Kristie and Morgan pretty hard. Maybe he'll open up soon.

I was walking to the house from the bunkhouse with Brock when a car comes barreling down the drive.

The car stops just inches from us. When the driver's side door opens, Brock and I look at each other and then back at the driver.

I walk up to her, "What the fuck do you want?"

The End

About the Author

Vic Leigh is an American Author and has worked in many fields throughout her life. She enjoys reading all authors, but romantic fiction and contemporary romance are her favorites. She a mother, grandmother, editor, and teacher. Her small-town romance books are hot, spicy, and addictive.

Keep up to date on new arrivals at all social media sites:

www.warrioresspublishing.com
www.vicleighbooks.com
www.facebook.com/vicleighbooks
www.tiktok.com/@vicleighbooks
www.instagram.com/vicleighbooks

Milton Keynes UK
Ingram Content Group UK Ltd.
UKHW020908050424
440683UK00001B/15